BELLA'S BOYS

A TALE OF COSMIC HORROR BY
THOMAS R CLARK

SNOWBLIND

Corey knew a foot of snow is one thing to behold, but dealing with it is another thing altogether. Walking through it is difficult, but the task can be managed. It's on par with walking through the shallows at a beach. You can drag your feet through it or raise each foot up and out of the depths. Either way, the end result is the same; it's inconvenient, slows you down some, and if you move too fast, it will trip you up.

Two feet of it is an entirely different story. Corey had discovered it's nearly fucking impossible. Two feet of snow comes up to, or over, an average person's knees. Walking through this is a chore, to put it mildly. Lifting your legs in the manner required to move through snow quickly tires a person out. Trappers and hunters long ago found the best way to deal with deep snow was to stay on top of it. Snowshoes, designed to displace the snow and support the wearer, would be the desired foot attire at this moment in time for anyone unlucky enough to be walking around in it ...

Bella's Boys: A Tale Of Cosmic Horror
Written By Thomas R Clark
Cover Art By Francois Vaillancourt
Interior Plate © 2018 By Mason Buchanan
Interior Design By Thomas R Clark
PREY FOR CHANGE art © 2020 by James P. McCampbell
Interior Art © 2020 by Erik Cullen
Interior art © 2023 by Deborah Coldiron
'The Scream,' 'Critical Mass' and 'Tara' created by John Skipp and Craig Spector. Used with permission.
Portions of the lyrics from Brothers and Freakshow appeared previously in: *A Book Of Light And Shadow,* published by Nightswan Press © 1999 & © 2018. Used with permission.

PUBLISHED BY
STITCHED SMILE PUBLICATIONS, LLC
© 2020
Second Edition © 2025
ISBN: 979-8-9991091-0-1

PRAISE FOR BELLA'S BOYS

"*The Thing* goes to karaoke" *Ronnie Dark – THE DARK*

"Claustrophobic and intricately paced." *Garret Cook – Author of Crisis Boy*

"Clark's created a small-town horror atmosphere that's twistedly absorbing." *Ryan Miller – Your New Opinion Podcast*

"A real mindfuck. Anchors the reader into a very specific moment and place in time...and then proceeds to pull on all the threads of reality around it." *Michael Kingston - writer/creator Headlocked*

"Sexy and stylish! Clark's slickly-told tale ranks among the best Lovecraftian-horror out there today!" *Pete Molnar – Author of Broken Birds*

"Clark uses music to set the era and the mood, like a soundtrack to bring the story to life." *Colin Delaney – AEW, ECW, 2CW & WWE Superstar*

"A sleek and well-written story." *Christine Morgan – SPLATTERPUNK AWARD WINNING author of Lake House Infernal*

ALSO BY THE AUTHOR

GOOD BOY
THE DEATH LIST
THE GOD PROVIDES
SUMMERHOME
A PRAYER FROM THE DEAD
IMMORAL DILEMMAS
WE ARE 13

COMING SOON

WHIRLWIND
THE CURSE OF KATIE ELDER
THE WITCH OF NOVEMBER
THE TELLING OF THE BEES

BELLA'S BOYS

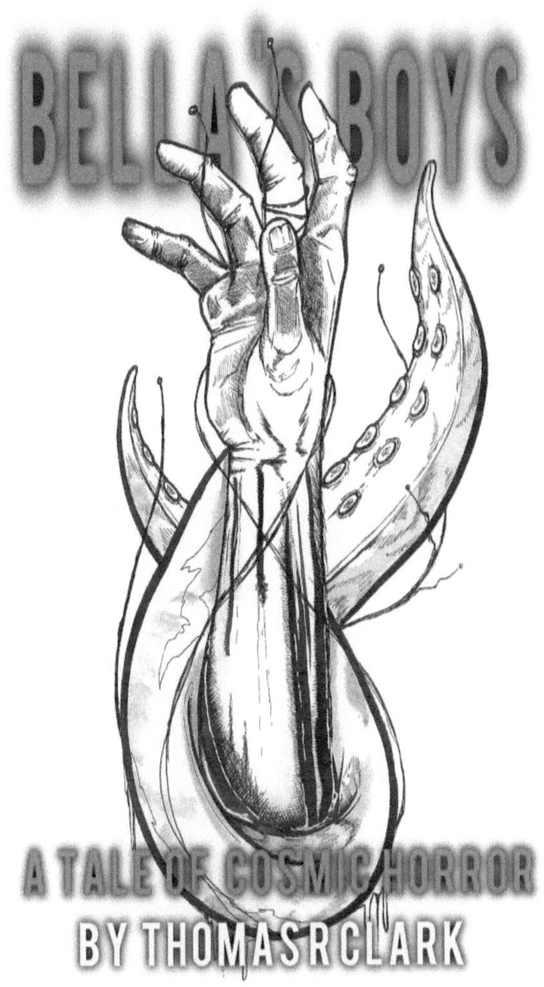

A TALE OF COSMIC HORROR

BY THOMAS R CLARK

STITCHED SMILE PUBLICATIONS
HOUSTON, TX

CHAPTER 1

**FRIDAY, MARCH 12, 1993 9:40 P.M.
RAFFERTY'S PUB, FENTON, NY
SNOWFALL: 0" ACCUMULATION (5" PACKED)**

Multicolored strobe lights flashed to the beat of the music. Hard and heavy, a blazing riff in E minor on a D tuned guitar resonated throughout the bar. Double kick drums machine-gunned in unison with a thunderous bass line. Corey Collins held his microphone in a grip of steel, his face making pained expressions in sync with the guitars blaring through the speakers around him on the bar's stage. His cue came, and he screamed the lyrics out, neck muscles flexing and cording from the stress as he sang in a high tenor.

Before him was a full bar of people, all from various parts of life, and each one entranced by his performance. He was a front man by trade and thus skilled in grabbing the attention of the masses. As the lead vocalist for a popular, regional hard rock touring band, Corey exercised these skills almost nightly for the last five years. The archetypes were all here. The blue-collar barfly who sat in the same stool every night, tired and drained but afraid to go home and be alone. The trio best friends on a girl's night out, leaving their husbands behind and pretending they're single right up until closing time. The guy with stage envy, singing along with every song, who wanted to be Corey. So forth and so on, a bar full of stereotypes, each with their own reason for being here.

Corey's eyes stopped scanning the crowd when he saw her, a diamond in a crowd of rough faces. The woman was sitting at the bar, watching him perform. Her face was a porcelain mask encircled by an obsidian cowl of long hair, with radiant emerald eyes and ruby lips. She looked delicate and fragile, but the pins and patches on her denim vest said otherwise. Heralding various bands from throughout the decades, the vest's accessories indicated she had sworn the blood oath at the altar of the Gods of Metal, making her hard as tempered steel.

Sing to me, lover, her eyes said. So Corey sang to her, and only her. The song ended, and applause burst out in the bar. He didn't acknowledge it. Instead, Corey hung onto the mic stand and bent his head in exhaustion, raising his eyes to see if she still watched him. She wasn't clapping. This discouraged him, but he smiled anyway as he stood up and reattached the microphone to the mic stand. She would be a challenge then. A moment passed, and he saw her turn and join the rest of the bar in their appreciation for his performance before turning her back to the stage.

•

core! He thought. He knew at this moment it wouldn't be a wasted trip to the shithole of upstate New York. He stood on a small stage in Rafferty's, an Irish dive bar. The bar had a new attraction called karaoke, supposedly a Japanese word for *tone deaf.* It played songs from popular bands without the vocals, complete with a video on a monitor providing the lyrics. Corey gave the bar patrons a little taste of what it was like to see him perform, even without his band tagging along.

"Give it up for Corey and his excellent rendition of 'One' from Metallica, ladies and gentlemen!" the DJ said, forcing another smaller round of applause. The portly middle-aged man had an eighties porn mustache and *Frankie* embroidered on his polo shirt. Corey had wondered about this guy all night. How did he do it? He'd proven to have a complete lack of trivial music knowledge, based on the comments he would make between singers. Oh, and the music in between the vocalists? Corey thought he was at a wedding.

In spite of all this going against him, Frankie had packed them in tonight. Corey shook his head in disbelief and walked offstage, making his way to the bar for another drink.

"Can I get Bobbie Be Good next? Bobbie Be Good singing '99 Red Balloons'!"

A heavy set Native American woman with long black hair walked up to replace Corey on stage. She wore a flannel top tucked into jeans pulled up far too high on her waist. Corey caught a whiff of Bobbie Be Good as she passed him on the dance floor.

Fenton's Finest, his internal monologue quipped, and was she ever, in a manner of speaking. *Fucking Fenton*. Corey shook his head.

The small city of Fenton, New York nested on a portion of the Onondaga Nation lands, north and west of Syracuse near the shores of Lake Ontario. The city's proximity to the Native American reservation lands provided a minority for local racists to focus their attention. Bobbie Be Good's ancestry wasn't giving Corey pause as they passed each other. The dichotomy she represented was another story. The woman was the complete opposite of his porcelain-masked goddess.

Bobbie Be Good was dirty, but not in a don't tell your mother, kinky sex kind of way. A vile, nose wrinkling stench emanated from her person. He noted her hair was a greasy sponge, littered with dander, an array of dead insects, dust bunnies and dried up who-knows-what.

For the love of God, how do you get bugs in your hair and not know?

The woman's body odor made him nauseous. He had a weak stomach. The smell of any garbage usually made him vomit, and this was pushing him over the edge. To top it off, it became obvious she wasn't wearing a bra. Her massive breasts swelled under the buttons of her shirt, threatening a wardrobe malfunction at any moment. Her shoulder bag seemed to be a Godsend. Its strap bisected her bosom, neatly separating and defining her breasts while holding back the stressed fabric. Corey silently prayed the strap and buttons would hold. Only the Lord knew if he would be able to contain himself, not completely sure if he'd laugh or vomit, if they burst out.

Sing for me.

"What?" Corey thought he heard Bobbie Be Good speak to him, but she was clearly surprised by his comment.

"I didn't say anything," she said. The last thing Corey wanted was to get stuck in a conversation with a backwoods hick covered in bugs and a desperate need for deodorant or skunk spray, anything to cover up her stench. He also didn't wish to be rude to the woman.

"Sorry, I didn't mean to startle you."

"It's okay. You're very good. You should sing in a band."

"I do, actually." Corey looked down, hoping dropping the eye contact would signal the end of their conversation.

"That's so awesome! I knew it! I told J.R., my boyfriend; he didn't think you did, but he was probably having a little green monster attack, ya know, he was jealous. He gets like that around guys that sing better than he does."

"I'll try not to make him jealous."

"Bobbie, you're up!" the DJ handed her the microphone, giving Corey the chance to get away.

Jealous? My fucking God!

The electronic Euro Pop synthesized sound of Nena grew in volume. Bobbie Be Good, who desperately needed a bra and a bath, also needed vocal lessons. She wailed into the microphone, out of key enough to set his inner ear off balance. Her performance set aside any concerns the singer may have had about karaoke stealing the spot of a good band. He threw a hand up and dragged it down over his forehead and his face before pinching it off at his chin.

I'm in hell, he thought. Then he saw her again, his goddess, and his thoughts came back to heaven. Her back was turned to him, her attention focused on something other than Bobbie Be Good's singing.

He finally reached the bar and found a seat next to his goddess had opened up. Corey edged in, not acknowledging her proximity, and thrust a hand forward. A ten-dollar bill extended from his fist, a banner to catch the bartender's attention. The barkeep, an older, balding gentleman with trembling limbs, hobbled to Corey. He smiled as if he knew Corey for years.

"Hi. Corey was it? Good job up there. I'm Al. What do you need?"

"Hi, Al. Thanks. I'll take a Blue and two shots of Jame-oh, please."

"Right away," the old man said and set about putting the order together.

"Two shots?" he heard a feminine voice speak up. It was his goddess, speaking to him. "Hitting the bottle a little hard tonight, are we?"

He smirked and raised an eyebrow. "It's less than a week from Saint Patty's Day, and I feel the need to celebrate this shitstorm the weatherman says is coming. I think it's bullshit, personally." He turned to face her. She was more beautiful close up. Her features were striking and flawless.

"I saw the satellite pictures on the news," she informed him. "The storm is bigger than the country. It spreads across half the Atlantic Ocean. It's kind of sexy, if you ask me."

"That's great. Doesn't help to make a buck tonight." He watched as Al placed a pair of shot glasses on the bar and poured the

Irish whiskey into each, "Besides, I've never believed a damn weather report my whole life, so let's drink to that!" Corey slid one of the shot glasses in front of her.

"I'll never say no to a free shot," she added, "but I love big storms like this. They turn me on. Something about being snowbound with nothing to do but fuck and listen to good music."

"I'll never say no to that!"

"I would hope not!"

"Cheers!" Corey toasted. In unison the pair slammed the shots back. A chorused sigh followed. Corey chased the fire with his cold beer, taking a large gulp from the long-necked brown bottle.

He placed his hand over his chest and quipped, "Milady, it was for your pleasure." He wondered, briefly, why he called her *milady*. He hadn't tried that pick-up line since seeing *The Princess Bride*. It failed miserably then.

"Thank you?" she asked more than told him. The cadence of her voice hypnotized him. She was ... *Royalty?* Corey's id kicked into gear and went overboard, pouring on the charm.

"You are very welcome, Milady. Do you sing, too? I saw you singing along with me earlier."

"Uh, no," she laughed. "I wasn't singing, I was lip syncing with the words on the big screen." She gestured to the bar's large television monitor airing the videos and lyrics for the patrons. "I wish I could sing. My voice makes water run back up the spigot in the shower. I actually own a karaoke machine, but I never use it. So, no, I don't sing. But I am here to find someone to sing for me."

"I find it hard to believe how someone as stunning as you could not have a voice like an angel." He paused for dramatic effect, then added, "Milady," and curtsied with his hand. He didn't think he was going too far. She was the only attractive woman in the bar with or without beer goggles. She deserved special attention.

"What is it with the Milady shit? Am I a damsel in distress, and you're my knight come to rescue me?"

"I could be. Maybe I've come to rescue you from a shit bar."

"Possibly. But where would you carry me off to? I hate to say it, but the weathermen are nailing this one on the head. We're getting dumped on. There's not many places you could take me."

"Does the lady have accommodations locally we could explore?"

"The lady's name is Sandy, but everyone calls me Bella."

"What a lovely, dangerous name."

"Bella Strega, I'm told."

"Ah, a beautiful witch?"

"You know Italian?"

"Some. My Mom and I moved to Canastota when I was ten. All Italians, onions, wrestling, and the International Boxing Hall of Fame."

"I think Italian is sexy."

"I'm all Irish, babe, just Italian by association."

"That's fine. This is what matters," she pointed at him. "You do music, and I like music. I like it hard; I like it fast ..." she traced the finger down his cheek. The nail sent a shiver through his body at her touch. *Don't go up to the chalkboard with a boner,* Dad would tell him. It was rare good advice he'd given his son, shortly before Corey's mother had thrown him out. At this moment, the younger Collins adhered to it.

"OK, does Bella live in Fenton? Cos I live in Syracuse, and that's too far away to drive with all I've drank tonight. Plus this karaoke machine you mentioned has struck up my curiosity."

"Corey, baby, you're in luck tonight. You see, not only do I have a karaoke machine, I've got an opening for a front man in my own private band."

"You know, I already sing for a band."

"You do? That explains why you're so good."

"Thank you," he blushed. *Why are you embarrassed? She's trying to pick you up!* He admonished himself before continuing, "In fact, I was supposed to have a gig up here tonight, at the Fenton Hotel, but the dirtbag owner canceled it. Said nobody would be going. For fuck's sake, it was Pat Stephenson's Remembrance party!"

"Isn't he the comedian who disappeared while on tour last year?"

"He sure is! Man I miss him. Here's a funny thing, him and I used to trade girlfriends in college. Fucked up he went and vanished. The bar would have been packed, storm or not."

"That's stupid. I was going to go there tonight. I prefer live bands. The only reason I'm here, well, is because the hotel is closed." This statement only confirmed Corey's suspicions. The place was filled with locals, many of whom were as pissed as he was the gig had been canceled. Well of Sorrow was always a sellout, and now the Fenton Hotel was empty, but Rafferty's was packed from one end of the bar to the other. His ego told him it was all because he had brought them here; it certainly couldn't be Frankie.

"See what I mean, man? I told Mac he was stupid." Corey shook his head.

"What band was yours on the bill?"

"Well of Sorrow."

"I can't say I've heard of the name before today. Are you new?"

"We've been around a couple years, we actually have a CD out. It's got a few good songs on it. We play in Fenton quite a bit, actually."

"I don't know about that, but I have my own band. It's called Bella's Boys. And I'm warning ya now, it's not of this world," she said, nodding in approval. "So will you sing for me?"

"You bet your ass I will."

"Then what are we waiting for? Put your name on the sign-up sheet."

Ignoring the almost painful erection in his tight jeans, Corey snagged a song book and looked for something to sing. He was getting low on material. Karaoke seemed to be limited in song choice, unless you preferred Elvis or country. He found a Night Ranger song, "Don't Tell Me You Love Me", a classic off their Dawn Patrol album. A moment later he was writing his name and the corresponding song number on a slip of paper. He brought it to the DJ, or rather KJ, for "karaoke jock," which he insisted on being called, as Bobbie Be Good was finishing her song. Frankie took the slip while cuing up Exposé's "Point of No Return" for the pleasure of the bar patrons. Some of the women in the bar started a small circle, dancing near the stage.

I want to be with you, baby.

Corey stopped in place, looked around to see who was singing along with Exposé in his ear, but no one was there. He found it odd. He went to move on but found his path to the bar and his heavy metal queen closed off.

The big Onondaga woman stopped right in front of Corey, blocking his exit, for the second time in a five-minute span. Her time on stage, under the lights, had ripened her malodor. Corey didn't think it was possible for a human to smell like a wet goat dipped in pig shit, but the karaoke singer had attained this dubious achievement.

"Got another one for me, Bobbie?" Frankie asked. Bobbie turned to look at the KJ.

"No, Frankie baby," her voice was as dull and out of key as her singing voice. How someone could *talk* out of key was beyond his comprehension. Bobbie was becoming a paradox of personality. "I've got to get home. Granny needs her diapers changed; I have to work at the Byrne tomorrow. And RJ has to work at the mall, so he has to get home."

Jesus, is she going to give us the whole itinerary? Why, for the love of God, did I need to know her grandmother is incontinent?

"Well, you be careful this weekend, it's going to get nasty out there."

This was too much. Corey's eyes were starting to water from her body odor. He felt the nausea returning, his mouth filling with lukewarm drool waiting to burst out from his lips.

"Yeah, it's gonna be, I can't wait!" Bobbie agreed, her body language reminded Corey of a toddler seeing a puppy for the first time. Her eyes were wide open, and an ear to ear grin exposed more of her dental work than Corey had ever hoped to see. Her banter reminded Corey of Barney the Dinosaur.

I smell you, you smell me, we're a disgusting family.

"Plus, you know how superstitious Granny is about the weather. When a storm like this comes, it's all about the *Hadiwennoda:dye's*. She thinks us singing tonight is going to make the storm worse."

Corey's mind was focusing on trying to translate the Onondaga word she had pronounced. Living in this region, Corey never got used to the tribal tongues. He found them to be a little too phonetic, and his translations were often far from their actual meaning.

Had a Wendy's? Had a Wendy's what? A never frozen burger? A baked potato? Or maybe a Frosty because of the weather?

"You know how old superstitious ladies can be set in their ways," Bobbie Be Good continued.

"She's a crazy old hoot," the KJ told her.

"Ah-hum-in-ah-whatsit-dye?" Corey said out loud. Bobbie turned her head so fast the husk of something dry and once alive fell out of her hair.

"Oh, hello again, Mr. Karaoke Band Man!" Corey cringed. She had given him a nickname, *"Hadiwennoda:dye's,* The Thunders. It's a tribal legend. They are Thunder and Lightning, benevolent sky spirits."

"Ho-kay then!" Corey did not want to be in this conversation. He turned his head and looked for Bella. She was still sitting on her stool. They made eye contact, and Corey felt his desire for his porcelain metal goddess grow.

"You're all good, Bobbie." Thankfully the KJ interrupted. "Tell RJ I said goodnight. I'll see you next week, Lord willing."

"Yeah, Frankie, Lord willing." Bobbie stepped away, clearing the air and opening a path for Corey to escape. He took a deep breath; Bobbie's musky aroma was lingering. Corey moved his ass, returning to the side of his porcelain skinned, heavy metal goddess. He saw another round of drinks waiting for him, Bella extending an arm to reserve his spot next to her.

This is going to be one hell of a night. Corey was certain. He felt rejuvenated by something, and as the night progressed, his second wind was in full overdrive. Or was it the company he kept? Regardless, whatever the reason, he fully expected to see the sun rise before he went to sleep.

•

Corey and Bella sat together at the bar and observed the patrons during the evening, enjoying the proximity of one another as they slowly became intoxicated on imported beer and Irish whiskey. Apparently, people watching was a hobby of hers. More often than not, Bella was spot on about the people they discussed. The singers all had pseudonyms they used while singing, and this practice carried on to the couple's private dissertation on Rafferty's clientele.

Sexy Suzie, who wasn't at all sexy, sang sad country songs. Her eyes said she'd suck your dick and tell on you, Corey believed. It soon became obvious she was cheating on her husband, knowing hubby would never step foot in a bar with karaoke.

Suzie's beau, Rockin Ron with Kung Fu Grip, resembled one of the old twelve-inch tall GI Joe dolls from the seventies. He came complete with a close-cropped beard, brush cut, and cupped hands gripping invisible beer bottles, or possibly dicks, Corey wasn't quite sure. One thing was certain, Rockin Ron with Kung Fu Grip sure sang a lot of Elvis.

Doctor Love was their favorite. She was what would happen if the girl with naturally curly red hair Charlie Brown was infatuated with grew into a lonely and homely woman who thought of herself as a diva vocalist. After singing her third Janis Joplin song through her nose, Corey knew she wouldn't last a single band practice with real musicians, but who was he to pass judgment on her.

Crooked Chuck, who literally had one leg longer than the other, refused to sing Bon Jovi and Billy Joel without any number of his friends joining him. This included Sideways Pete, who shuffled about the bar with a wobbly gait, and One-Legged Tony, who would air guitar with his prosthetic leg during guitar solos in songs. Bella dubbed them Crooked Chuck and The Hitchhikers, and Corey toasted this with a double shot of whiskey.

Darling Nikki sang guy songs, classic rockers from Styx and Foreigner and the like. She was covered in tattoos, and was sexy enough, Corey noticed, from the neck down. From the neck up, she was a Greek gorgon, ready to turn anything but your pecker to stone.

"She looks like Geddy Lee from Rush," Bella quipped after the woman left the stage.

Corey's father would have told him to put a flag over her face and fuck her for Old Glory. More great advice to give a pre-teen.

The most bizarre, hands down, was Big Daddy Vick, who sang the blues and gyrated like Elvis. Except BDV weighed close to four hundred pounds and his gut hung out from under his polo shirt. He sounded like Peter Boyle's version of 'Putting on the Ritz' from *Young Frankenstein* every song he sang. But with his sunglasses and fedora, the ladies of Fenton seemed to adore him.

Karaoke was, without a shadow of a doubt, a unique, cliquey culture. Each singer had their quirks and idiosyncratic mannerisms.

Then there were the spectators, the bar patrons too afraid to participate in public speaking, which is essentially what karaoke is. They were as interesting and quirky as the singers themselves, and just as supportive or vain.

Corey couldn't help but laugh when he overheard Doctor Love make snide remarks to her clique of friends, mocking Sexy Suzie's singing. The doctor was the only real singer out of a half dozen people. The others were either too scared, or too sober to get anywhere near a microphone.

Frankie had to pull his song books and stop taking sign-ups shortly after midnight. Even then he ran over the two a.m. cut off time by ten minutes. Al turned the lights on and kept pointing at his wrist. The KJ shrugged his shoulders in response.

When the last singer, a handicapped Irishman who went by the moniker Pistol Paull With Two L's finished an enthusiastic rendition of "Johnny B. Good", Frankie killed the house music.

"Great job, Paull! Give it up for Pistol Paull!" As soon as Pistol had turned his back and walked off the stage, Frankie announced, "If you don't work here or fuck somebody who works here, go home and fuck somebody, but not here!"

People started milling out of the pub, a herd of sheep exiting their stockade.

"I guess this is our cue to jet," Corey said to Bella.

"I guess so," she agreed. "I don't feel much like driving; how are you?"

"I think I can handle it. How far are you from here?"

"Not far. A few blocks, actually."

"Oh, good." He slammed one last shot of Irish whiskey, washed it away with his remaining beer. "I should be drunk and unable to operate a motor vehicle in about fifteen minutes, so how about we beat it?" She nodded, he took her hand, and the duo joined the parade of patrons exiting the premises.

CHAPTER 2

SATURDAY, MARCH 13, 1993 2:16 A.M.
305 PARK ST., FENTON, NY
SNOWFALL: 0"

Corey drove his cherry red Cavalier. It was clear out, still not a flake of snow to be found. The streets were empty, too. Earlier in the day it had been a different story. The weathermen had been scaring every living person within earshot of a television or radio with warnings of impending meteorological doom. People were out in droves to buy out every Wegman's grocery store in the county. He couldn't get as much as a case of beer on the way up here tonight. Milk, bread, bottled water or eggs? Good luck. The shelves were picked clean. Not even a bag of fucking potato chips.

Bella's house wasn't far from the bar. She sat in the front, next to him, as calm and reserved as she'd been all night. A shot down the main drag, take a left by the bank, and there you were. The lot at 305 Park Street held a small, unassuming raised ranch with an attached garage. It was nestled in the middle of the street, between two other identical properties. The remnants of a snowier than normal winter—about half a foot of snow pack—decorated the front lawns of each house.

Gray asbestos shingles rendered the place almost invisible in the darkness. A short driveway stretched in front of the garage. With its door closed, the garage resembled a boxed skull, the windows appearing as a pair of square eyes staring him down. White trim neatly defined its facial features. The handle was a nose, the bottom panels a toothy mouth. He'd seen things buzzed before, but not this vivid. It freaked him out so much, he turned off the car lights before coming to a complete stop.

Once inside the house, Bella locked the door behind them and left the lamps off. Her demeanor changed. She grabbed him by the waist, pulled him close and kissed him. Her tongue snaked into his mouth, twirling about. Locked in her embrace, Corey saw shadows of muted light shone through the sheer curtains adorning the bay window in the living room. Aside from a large entertainment center and bookshelf, a sofa, loveseat, and armchair were the only pieces of furniture in an otherwise bare living area.

They disrobed one another, still kissing and fondling as they went, letting the clothing fall where it may. He didn't hesitate to bend her over the arm of the loveseat and slap her ass.

Harder.

He heard her say, so he slapped her cheeks harder. His hand cracked against her skin. She thrust back at him and gyrated against his crotch. His dick, already stiffened from arousal, slid up and down between her cheeks. He was about to pull back and enter her, when she stood up, turned around and initiated a long deep kiss. Corey knew he wasn't in love, this was lust, but damn they felt the same.

She paused long enough to move away and turn her five-disc CD player on shuffle, changing between Anthrax, The Scream, Masters Of Reality, The Dark, and Metallica, of course. She was truly a metal goddess with great, eclectic tastes.

Corey took a moment to soak in her beauty. He'd never been with a woman so perfect before, and here, in Fenton, New York, of all the fucking places in the world to be. She was indeed a beautiful witch.

Suddenly, the whiskey and beer cocktail party hit Corey in the gut, starting a fight of epic proportions. It was the Irish sons of John Jameson versus the Canadian boys of John Labatt, and the Canadians were kicking the Irish out. He felt bile rising in his throat. His mouth watered with a warm, smooth spittle he knew heralded the imminent evacuation of the contents of his stomach.

"Where's your bathroom?" He managed to ask without spitting up.

"Over there, lover," Bella pointed to a closed door, obscured by the shadows, "the light switch is on the wall, behind the door." He broke away from his metal goddess and followed her direction, holding in a mouthful of spit and digestive fluid in his mouth as it burned his tongue and the back of his throat. He didn't bother to turn on the light, afraid it would make things worse.

He closed the door behind him. Corey fell to his knees at the base of her toilet, sweat beading on his forehead and brow. He spit out the contents of his mouth and hung his head over the bowl. A nonstop stream of drool poured from his bottom lip. He swayed to and fro, dripping onto the toilet seat and the tile flooring.

"... *hello* ..."

Corey heard a soft voice speak in the room with him. Catching himself, he stood straight up, looking for the source. He wiped his chin with a free hand and held himself erect with the other, holding himself up with the shower curtain. He reached a vertical base faster than he had anticipated, making him dizzy. Moonlight pierced the bathroom window. He pushed aside the shower curtain, expecting to find a jilted lover standing in the tub. It was empty.

He felt the urge to urinate, so he pulled apart his button fly Levi's and started to piss. His stream split, and sprayed the back of the toilet seat cover with urine while sprinkling the seat itself.

Fuck! He thought to himself and remembered his manners through his drunken haze. *Lift the seat, asshole,* his voice of reason commanded. The wooden seat cover clanked against the porcelain tank.

"... *here ... join ... come* ..."

Corey heard the voice again, distinct and clear. He twisted his head to the left and right. There was no one in the small bathroom with him. He didn't think Bella would be pranking him. He wondered if someone was standing outside the window. Corey peered through and saw nothing but the street. The urge to vomit came upon him again. He turned and dropped to his knees again, worshiping the figurative porcelain altar in Bella's bathroom.

He was greeted by a black slime, about an eighth of an inch thick, coating the rim of the toilet bowl. Glutinous, with hairs and pieces of bathroom tissue speckled throughout, the ichor shimmered in the moonlight.

Then there was the stench. The slime reeked of piss, mildew, decaying fish and rotted vegetables. By comparison, Bobbie Be Good smelled of roses. He'd seen dirty toilets before, but this was unheard of.

Did she ever lift the fucking seat and clean it? Mortified and disgusted all at once, his constitution had reached its breaking point, but Corey held back the bile and viscous saliva filling his jowls. There was no way he was putting his face near the filth, the creeping fucking crud. Corey reached behind himself, found something cotton and stretchy hanging on the door, and blindly wiped the bowl clean. Relieved, he let go of the elastic cloth, it sprang out his hand, back into its place. Corey let it all out. The Irish, the

Canadians, and all their friends were purged from his body.

The opening riffs to The Dark's "Full Balloon" echoed through the house. The song was an epic homage to the Balloon Boy murders off their *Don't Be Afraid Of* album. Inspired by the true story of mass murderer Patrick Dermotty, who roofied his classmates during a sleepover with lime Kool-Aid. Dermotty then proceeded to make balloon animals out of their eviscerated intestines as they lay helpless on the floor.

It made quite an appropriate soundtrack, Corey thought, for the activity at hand. Ronnie Dark's signature guitar penetrated the thin bathroom door as Corey vomited, mercifully covering the sounds of his retching.

"*Drink the Kool Aid!*" The Dark's vocalist, Steve Brodie, chanted in rhythm with the guitars.

Corey screeched as the contents of his stomach continued to exit his body, harmonizing with the song.

"*Drink the Kool Aid!*" His diaphragm spasmed, causing a dry heave and comedic Jerry Lewis sounding noises.

"*Drink the Kool Aid!*"

"... sing ..."

He stopped, his diaphragm convulsing. The voices, he heard them again, under the music as he stood up. This was too much. He went to the sink, turned on the water, washed his face and rinsed his mouth. He found a tube of toothpaste, squeezed an ample amount onto his forefinger and brushed his teeth and tongue with it. He gagged and almost spasmed back into vomiting, dry heaving as the minty paste mixed with bile and regurgitated alcohol. Finally, satisfied he was presentable, Corey exited the dark bathroom. The door behind him latched closed as the song built to an orchestral climax.

"... sing ... for ... me ..." the voice said when *They* were finally alone, creeping up Bella's nightgown on the door. Corey had unwittingly removed *Them* from *Their* hiding spot on the toilet.

.

Corey staggered back into the living room, winning the fight to regain his composure and remain vertical. *Throw up and you feel better, son,* his Dad told him once before. Though it often was the case, just as often it was not. Particularly when booze was involved.

He found Bella, still naked, beckoning him with an outstretched hand to join her in the adjacent bedroom.

Come to me, lover, Corey thought he heard her say, but he couldn't tell over the volume of the music. They embraced and fell back onto her bed. She held him in the small of his back with one hand and guided him into her with the other. She was warm and soothing, and oh so wet and welcoming. They slowly built a rhythm to the music as he slid in and out of her.

Corey's balls were slapping off Bella's ass when she put her ankles behind his neck and pulled him in deeper. The latest Anthrax album, with the guy from Armored Saint singing about the Black Lodge from Twin Peaks, blared from the CD player. Then it was The Scream and The Dark, again. Each song blended into another, setting the perfect rhythm for their coitus with each changing track.

Bella's feet held him in place, a sexual vice grip Corey couldn't escape from if he wanted to. Her toes tickled his cheeks. Corey wasn't a foot guy. He never had been. He couldn't remember who first told him feet were nasty. It might have been his father, whose repertoire of poor advice was the least example of his horrible parenting before Mom had enough of his philandering and sent him packing. Dad had also told him to make sure he found a girl who gave good head, because you'll never get her pregnant.

"Yuck, yuck yuck!"

So why did Corey feel the urge to suck on Bella's toes?

He sucked on her feet, finding they were delicious. Her eyes opened wide. She gripped him harder, pulled him in tighter. He looked down at the raven headed goddess, sweat dripping off his forehead onto her chest, splashing off her tits. They'd been at it for at least an hour, and she hadn't made a single sound, not the slightest moan. There was no doubt she was enjoying their intimacy, but now, as he thought of it, Corey realized the woman, who had talked his ear off in the bar, hadn't made a peep at all since they started banging. She only smiled, as she did now, albeit in the throes of ecstasy from their lovemaking.

"Come for me, baby," she finally spoke. The words tickled the base of his spine, sending a jolt down to his scrotum. His balls retracted, and Corey couldn't hold back any longer. He let loose inside of her, filling her up. Corey arched his back and pushed into her as far and as hard as he could as he ejaculated. His tip found her cervix, the sensations overwhelming him into a full-body shudder. Finally spent, he collapsed next to her on the bed. They lay there for some time, not moving. Two straight hours of fucking had exhausted the duo. Corey had started to doze off when she moved.

"I'll be right back, lover." She kissed him on the forehead and excused herself from the bedroom. Corey sank into the blankets and pillows. When he felt her return, he'd started to drift off into sleep, his mind semi-lucid. She nested into his arms; the pair spooned together. As they drifted off to sleep, Corey thought he heard the voices again as the dreams and nightmares took over.

"... sing ..."

•

Corey's mind fell back to the bar. He was sitting on a stool watching Sexy Suzie and Rockin Ron sing "I Got You Babe," flirting away. Because Ron was over a foot taller than Suzie, he sang the song on his knees, doing his best impression of Sonny Bono. Suzie, in turn, mimicked

Cher's monotone wail with amateur grace. Bella was next to him.

"Dance with me."

Corey stood with her, embracing his porcelain skinned romantic interest. They danced, twirling together through the bar's dance floor. Before his inner, dreaming eye, the room was spinning. Corey rose up, out of Bella's arms, and hovered above the room. The bar was gone, replaced by Bella's bedroom.

Below him, he saw his naked body embracing Bella. Her legs wrapped around his hips, holding his physical form. Her flesh seemed to meld with his, and he couldn't distinguish between her body and his own.

He realized he was trapped in an expanding bubble as the walls revolved about him, moving faster and faster until a vortex grew. Corey bobbed in the middle, teetering about, unable to find a center of balance.

"... sing ... for ... US ... SING ..."

The voice spoke, and it splintered into many. The words emanated from everywhere and moved with the vortex. Corey looked up.

Above him was a great expanse of blue and white, curving on a radius. Stars shone on the horizon, twinkling as they shimmered in place. Corey felt his being float up into the void. Behind him, Bella's bedroom ceased to be. There was only the void, beckoning his astral form. Corey saw it all, and nothing, in conjunction. The vortex widened, and Corey found himself inside the void.

"… join … US … be … US …"

Corey's mind fell into the void as the previous day flashed before him. It was a cold March night; the sky was clear and not a flake of snow could be found in the air. Well of Sorrow was on a stage, performing "Brothers," a song off their first CD, *Leave the Chicken.* The power ballad's hooky chorus and lamenting lyrics rang through an empty building. Corey sang, the words crying from his lips and lungs.

We weren't brothers; we were friends.

It's sad to know I won't see you again.

We weren't brothers, we were friends.

I wish we'd been closer, in the end.

Corey saw himself strut about the stage singing the song. The Double Ds, Drew and Dave and their dueling lead guitars, moving in synchronization. Johan standing to the side, swaying to the music, finger picking the strings on his bass, while Jimmy the human metronome kept them in time on his lavish drum kit.

The song ended and the image of Mac Dixie, owner of the Fenton Hotel, shimmered and shook in the air before him.

"Gotta cancel the gig tonight due to the weather, nobody gave a shit about Pat anyhow." Echoed from his vibrating lips. *"Besides, it's the storm of the century!"*

The voices chanted this over and over, the vocalizations wasting no time building into a surround sound crescendo. The bar, his bandmates, and the bar owner disintegrated into a flurry of snow, and Corey found himself once again listing in the void.

"... storm ... century ..."

Translucent, aeriform jellyfish floated past Corey's body. Their tentacles fluttered about, tasting the ether. One errant tendril touched Corey's fingertip and looped around it, holding the digit tight. He pulled his hand back, but the jellyfish's grasp was solid, and Corey found his body moving toward it instead of away.

No, oh no, oh no! Corey felt his heart rate increase as the tentacle pulled him closer and closer to the jellyfish. He opened his mouth to cry for help.

No words came out.

More tentacles reached from the jellyfish, latching onto his extremities, holding them in an iron grip.

The creature engulfed Corey's entire being.

"... *US ... join ... with ... US ...*"

Then he heard it, the music, pulsing through the jellyfish's body. It was a familiar tune, one Corey swore he heard before. It was a combination of every great eighties metal song, it was every song and none, all at once. Less the words. The only words Corey heard came from another place, and they were stuck on repeat.

"... *sing ... US ... sing ... for ... US ... join ... US ...*"

He felt a sense of weightlessness within the jellyfish. Something was growing within, expanding ever outward. Corey found his body spread across the top of the bubble, pushing him ever outward to the edge of the void. He felt the pressure all over his body. He was simultaneously being stretched and crushed.

"... *SING ...*"

It burst.

"… FOR …"

Corey felt his body rendered to pieces.

"… US!"

Darkness and void, Corey's mind shut off, no longer able to process the madness unfolding in his dreamscape.

•

Corey woke to the sun shining on his face. At first he forgot where he was. *Bella.* He was at Bella's house, a chick he'd met at the karaoke bar, and he was in Fenton. The air in the bedroom was dry and crisp and slightly cold. He felt about the bed, looking for his lover, but she was not to be found. Then he smelled it. Bacon.

She's cooking me breakfast. Nice! Corey thought. He stood up and stretched. She had given him a workout last night, and he still felt the aftershocks. The girl was a sex machine. His muscles ached, his groin was tender and sensitive to the touch. He pulled on his boxers and before he stepped out of the bedroom, noticed the posters of various metal bands adorning the walls. He hadn't seen them last night with the lights out. She was a true metalhead goddess. He made his way through the house and followed his nose to the kitchen.

Aside from the furniture, her living room held a 20-inch TV, a compact stereo system, and a sofa. A bookshelf was filled with CDs and books on New Age spirituality. He thumbed through the contents of the shelves. Her music tastes were, without a doubt, impeccable. He wasn't at all surprised to find the crystal and astrology books, some of them old and yellowed by time. Bella had quite the collection of weird. He moved on, following the scent of the fried pork back.

Bella stood in the kitchen in front of the stove, a black cotton and lace nightie barely covering her body. She was a thing of majestic beauty, even slaving over a hot stove. The fabric hugged her rounded curves, accentuating every inch it concealed. Corey wanted more of her, his cock was a throbbing divining rod, urging him in her general direction.

"Good morning, lover," she said without turning her head. "I knew this would wake you up."

"It did." He stepped behind her and wrapped his arms around her waist. He nuzzled her mane of black hair, pushing his nose into her locks and closed his eyes. He was rock hard and his groin rubbed against her buttocks. She pushed back, forcing the issue.

There was no going back. He hiked her nightgown up and released himself from his boxers. She didn't resist as he slid into her from behind. He couldn't get enough of this chick. His goddess. They groaned in unison. The walls of her vagina grasped his cock, milking the underside of his shaft along her pelvis bone from the base to the frenulum, forcing him to orgasm almost immediately. He stood within her, spent yet still stiff, holding her by the hips.

"... sing ..."

"What was that?" Corey jumped back, pulling out of her. He thought he heard it again, and it made his dick go soft on cue. That voice. He couldn't have, though. The voice wasn't real. He shook his head, desperately hoping it would remove the crazy causing him to hear shit.

"What?" Bella turned around, tongs for turning the bacon brandished in one hand, tugging on his now flaccid member with the other. "I asked you if you wanted to sing karaoke later." He shook his head. Now he was really hearing things. Talk about a buzzkill.

"Sorry, I'm a little hung over. Sure, I'll sing, after we eat. Let me pee."

He excused himself and found the bathroom, this time fully lit and far less imposing. He closed the door. It slammed with a crack as a collection of belts hanging from a hook whipped the hardwood. He shrugged, pissed, and washed his hands. All without hearing the voice.

I was doing some hardcore drinking last night if I was hearing shit and having fucked up nightmares, he thought. Pink Floyd's legendary light show, or even Triumph's, had nothing on whatever fucked up shit he was seeing in his sleep. He was surprisingly refreshed, all things considered. Shaking his head in bewilderment, Corey dried his hands on a towel and looked out the window. Snow was everywhere.

A half a foot of it had fallen sometime between when he fell asleep and now, and was still falling. Bella's house sat at the base of a hill with a steep incline. It was no surprise, then, to find a main road traversing the hill. A CENTRO City bus from Syracuse was currently attempting to pull a Little Engine That Could on the hill and failing miserably. He watched as it inched up the incline, the wheels slipping as they searched for traction. It stopped, only to slide uncontrollably back down. The bus came dangerously close to fishtailing before coming to a stop at the base, causing a gasp to rise from Corey.

Damn, that's gotta suck, he thought. He turned from the window and exited the bath. When he returned to the kitchen, Bella was serving the bacon on plates with toast and sunny-side-up eggs.

"Is this okay for your eggs?" She asked him.

"Sure is. I like dipping my toast in the yolk."

"Good." She smiled, content he was pleased with the meal. They ate in silence. Corey devoured the thick cut bacon, making little finger sandwiches which he dipped in the yellow yolk. He remembered more advice his Dad had given him, a week or so before Mom had thrown him out. *Don't forget son, eggs are nothing but hen cum. Yuck, yuck, that almost rhymed!* Johnny Collins had been the ultimate example of parenting gone wrong. You simply do not say certain things to a nine-year-old. Corey looked at the remaining fried eggs whites and had second thoughts about finishing his plate. Like the foot thing. None of this was the best advice to give to a pre-teen boy. Dear *wherever-he-went* Dad was full of shit, but when it came to feet and eggs, he might have been right. They were gross. Corey had been with his share of strippers over the years to reinforce this belief. Jamming your feet into those shoes created gnarled and twisted toes. Corey had Bella's toes in his mouth last night. His appetite was gone.

"That was great, thank you." He set his plate aside. She saw he hadn't eaten all his eggs.

"What, you didn't like it?"

"Oh, I did very much, but I'm full." He lied, patted his belly and smiled.

"Looks like we're snowed in, lover."

"Yeah, it does, but I really gotta try to get back to Syracuse today. I didn't leave enough food out for my cat," Corey lied. He hated cats.

"You sure you want to try the drive? It's pretty bad out."

"Really, I do need to try and go. Poor Mr. Whiskers"—he made up a name—"will never forgive me if I starve him to death."

"I think he'd be dead, if that was the case." She had sound logic. Corey couldn't argue it.

"Do you think cats have nine afterlives, too?" he joked back.

"I don't much care for cats, personally."

"Well, you probably don't want to eat any Chinese food from Solvay then."

"Why would I go to Solvay for Chinese when we have three restaurants here in Fenton?" She was serious. Corey wondered if she was a little touched. Sober Corey wasn't finding her to be as much of a porcelain goddess as drunk Corey had. Without her makeup, she was still attractive, but he wasn't fond of the way she looked at him. It was as if she was mentally devouring him with her eyes, and it made him uncomfortable.

"Never mind," he said. It wouldn't be worth it. "Thanks for breakfast, Bella, you outdid yourself."

"You don't know the half of it, lover." She walked over to him and held him tight, kissing Corey long and slow. It stirred his manhood. He thought about round four with Bella until he heard the fucking voice again. It made his blood run as cold as the snow outside.

"*... US ... sing ...*"

"I've really got to go," he pushed away from Bella. She pouted, her hands dropping to her hips, and tilted her head to the side. He didn't care. He was still hearing shit, and he had to go, a foot of snow or not.

"But you promised me you'd sing karaoke for me."

"Maybe next time?"

"Yeah," she conceded. Bella looked physically shaken by his desire to leave.

"Do you have a shovel?"

"In my garage. I'll get it for you." The two separated and Corey proceeded to get dressed.

CHAPTER 3

SATURDAY, MARCH 13, 1993 2:17 P.M.
305 PARK ST., FENTON, NY
SNOWFALL: 10"

The snow continued to fall as Corey struggled. Digging his car out of the driveway proved a futile exercise. He wasn't dressed for it, which made the job all the more difficult. He wore a jean jacket combined with a hooded sweatshirt, Levi's, a Well of Sorrow t-shirt and high top sneakers. This ensemble did not make for proper snow removal attire. He had gloves, but his fingers tore through the knitting an hour into the job. He was fighting a losing battle.

The plow had been by three times and each time it had built a taller wall of snow and ice at the base of the driveway. When Corey finally reached the driveway opening, half a dozen yards and two hours later, the three-foot-high wall was near impenetrable. The short length of driveway between Bella's garage doors and the street had filled with snow midway up to the tires on Corey's Cavalier. He cursed to himself. Then, unable to contain it any longer, out loud, at the world.

"Fuck you, plow man!" He threw a middle finger up in the air. The yarn covering his finger split as the glove stretched, exposing the tip. Corey kicked the snowbank. His leg sank deep into the mass and stuck there.

"Wonderful!" he cried out, trying to pull out his foot without removing his sneaker. He was successful, but snow traveled up his pant leg. He was soaked from the knees down and afraid of hypothermia, but he had to get this done.

Corey took a break and started his car, cranked the heat as high as it would go while he let the car idle. He soaked up the heat, looked at the big bay window of Bella's house, and saw her watching him. She'd been watching him the whole time. Not once did she ask if he needed help. She just sat there, watching him work. This irritated Corey. She could have offered a hand. But outside, out here, he didn't hear the voices, and he didn't have a boner. If he were inside with her, he feared it would be quite the opposite.

When he had sufficiently warmed his core, he set back outside to finish the job. He could barrel through the new snowfall no problem. If he could cut a big enough path through the snow, he'd be able to get out on the street and be on his way.

Bella chose this time to come outside to help, finally. Or so Corey thought. She was wearing the same outfit she'd been in at the bar. Tight jeans, a Dark tour shirt and her patched and pinned vest. It didn't surprise him to see the woman wasn't exactly dressed for the occasion.

"Having fun yet, lover?" she asked Corey.

"Does it look it? Nice of you to join me. I could've used a hand an hour ago."

"I had cleaning to do, sorry."

I hope you started by lifting the seat on your gross fucking toilet, he thought, then said aloud, "All done now?"

"Mostly. The snow is beautiful, isn't it? The flakes, each one looks the same when they float around in the air, yet they're different when you look at them up close. They're like people, you know. You're all different. Are you sure you want to leave?"

"Yes, I'm sure. I've got to get home to Mr. Whiskers." He continued the lie.

"But the snow! Don't you love it?"

"No," Corey shook his head, "it's a pain in the motherfucking ass is what it is."

"It turns me on like you wouldn't believe. Wanna make snow angels with me?"

"No, Bella, I really have to get this shoveled out so I can get on the road before nightfall." Corey knew with the weather and the cloud cover from the storm, darkness would set in sooner. He didn't have time to fuck around.

"You're no fun!" Bella took her vest and t-shirt off. Her tits burst out.

"What the fuck are you doing?"

"What does it look like?" She kicked off her boots, pulled her jeans off, and stood nude in the snow. Steam poured off Bella's body, creating a fog about her. Corey couldn't believe she had actually stripped outside during a blizzard in the middle of the day. He felt his lust starting to rise again at the sight of her nakedness.

She fell back onto a snowbank, extended her arms and legs and proceeded to create a snow angel in the bank. It was erotic, if nothing else. Corey held back the urge to strip and mount her on the snow bank. Satisfied with her performance, Bella stood up, smiling, her eyes wide open in awe.

"Look!" She pointed. "My bum made an imprint!" Corey had to admit, she planted a nice ass print into the bank. "Your turn!"

"No, Bella! I have to go. Put your clothes back on. Somebody is going to call the cops on you."

"Nobody can see us, Corey. The snow visibility is next to nothing." He couldn't argue this. Standing as near his car as they were, he now saw he couldn't see the end of the driveway, let alone any of the neighbors' homes. She jumped the snowbank onto the lawn and fell back. White powder erupted into the air from the impact, and Bella disappeared in the snow.

Jump in with me, Corey, he heard her from under the blanket of snow.

"No! You're going to catch a cold!" he said and returned to the task of shoveling out the end of the driveway.

No I won't. Come back inside with me. Your cat will be fine.

Corey ignored her. A few moments later he heard her front door open and close. He looked back and saw Bella had indeed gone back inside. He was about two feet into the side of the bank when a DPW dump truck with massive, steel plow blades painted orange came up his side of the street, a load of road salt carried inside. The giant blade and over-hanging wing cleared the road of snow and spread a secondary blizzard to either side of it.

"Don't you fucking dare, you bastard!" Corey swore as he jumped back as far as he could. Fear of being buried by the snow the blade was expelling had him go back even further, to the hood of his Cavalier. The plow reached the property line, dropped its wing blade and cleared him out.

"Motherfucker!" Corey screamed in elation. He looked up to see if Bella was still watching from the window. She was. He waved goodbye but didn't wait to see if she waved back. He hopped in his car, gave it a few revs of the engine and burst forward onto the road in an explosion of white powder.

Snow is a son of a bitch, Corey was learning. Shoveling the shit for two hours was only his initiation. The road was slick, and the snow created a frictionless plane for tires to spin on. The snow fell nonstop, creating whiteout conditions and no visibility. The wheels of Corey's Cavalier spun as they sought traction. The snow fell fast and covered the roads, already a thick pack of ice.

He kept the car in second and slowly made his way down Park Street, turning the wheel as needed to stay in motion. He got past Key Bank and down to the main drag and told himself this wasn't so bad. Across the street, a Byrne Dairy convenience store with gas pumps sat next to a Fay's Drug store. He could barely see the yellow of the giant Fay's sign through the falling snow. Visibility was still near to nothing. The latter was closed, but the gas station was open. Corey noted he had half a tank of gas, not good in weather conditions of this magnitude. He cut the wheel and slid, literally, into the Byrne Dairy parking lot, coming to a stop next to the pumps.

The lot was a slushy mix of road salt and ice. He could taste the salt on the air, mixing with the sickly-sweet carbon monoxide of the car exhaust. It watered his eyes as much as it drew snot from his nose. He almost slipped in the slick mixture, which succeeded in soaking through his sneakers. He'd been successful at keeping them dry while shoveling for nearly three hours. He shook his head and opened the door to the convenience store.

He stopped short and did a double take after entering, but his eyes hadn't deceived him. Sure as shit, Bobbie Be Good was behind the counter, or at least she resembled the karaoke singer. This woman was cleaner, slimmer and prettier. He questioned his perceptions then, as he'd heard of beer goggles making women prettier as the night went on but never the opposite. She couldn't be the Bobbie Be Good from last night. But her eyes. Corey never forgot a person's eyes, and she had Be Good's green eyes.

Her name badge proudly declared her name to be Roberta Webster, confirming at least part of the assumption. Corey hoped it would have been something a little more indicative of her, something more Native American, like Bobbie-Smells-Like-Turtle-Shit or something along that line. He found his way to the cooler, dug out a Pepsi and brought it to the counter.

"I remember you!" She was bursting with joy and recognition, "You're Karaoke Band Man from last night at Rafferty's!"

Corey's face turned red, embarrassed; the nickname she had bestowed upon him had stuck. He was relieved no one else was in the store at this moment. The clerk was indeed Bobbie Be Good. She rang up the soda, and Corey dug a twenty dollar bill out of his pocket. "The soda and put the rest on," he looked out the store's window, but couldn't make out the pump number he sat in front of.

"Pump two," she completed his sentence. Bobbie didn't smell as bad as she had the night before. He noted her hair looked clean. She even seemed a few pounds lighter. *Everything* was different about her. Though she still pulled her pants up far too high about her waist, now she was thankfully wearing a bra under a shirt less likely to burst at its seams.

"That will leave you $18.89 for the gas."

"So much for a ninety-nine cent soda, hah? Nothing is truly ninety-nine cents anymore, is it? Damn taxes. The government is out to get us, I swear."

"Tell me and my people about it. We've been fucked over by the white man for five hundred years." The expletive caught him off guard. She seemed too nice to cuss.

"Ain't that the truth, sister," Corey said. He realized Bobbie wasn't half bad of a person. He felt horrible for mocking her the night before, even if it'd been subconsciously.

"I mean, they gave the Indians on Manhattan like twenty-five bucks in baubles for the island. That would be like me offering you my fake diamond earrings for your car and you saying yes."

"It's fucked up; I hear ya! I remember hearing you mention your grandmother last night. Is she a Medicine Woman?" Bobbie's smile left her face, replaced by a stern scowl.

"Medicine Woman? Why not Medicine Squaw, while you're at it? It's just as racist." She unclasped one of the earrings and slapped it on the counter. "Got the title to that Cavalier on you?"

"You're fucking kidding, right?" Corey asked. She said nothing, her face stoic.

She maintained the ruse as long as she could. Bobbie's eyes grew as wide as her grin. "I'm just kidding." She tripped over her words a little, trying to repress her laughter. Corey was relieved and sighed aloud.

"Hah, hah, hah. Sorry, I don't mean to sound racist, I just—" he started to defend himself, but Bobbie cut him off before he could dig a bigger hole and tell her how many Onondaga friends he has.

"It's okay. You don't, Mr. Karaoke Band Man. She's a tribal historian, though, and wanted me to become one. But I like singing too much. Say, what band are you in again?"

"Well of Sorrow. We're based down in Syracuse."

"Nice. I'll have to check you out sometime. Do you have a CD?"

"We do, but I don't have any with me, I'm sorry." They were with the merch, in Jimmy's van in Syracuse. "Next time I'm up here I'll bring you one."

"I'm a singer, too, you know."

"You are?"

"I've got a CD, too."

"Oh, do you?" This revelation spiked Corey's curiosity. How was it a woman whose vocalizations reminded him of a sick dog trapped in a drainage ditch could make a CD? She dug into her purse and produced a jewel case. It was her on the cover, wearing a white leather jumpsuit decorated with tassels and rhinestones. In a bold point font emblazoned above her head was the title *Bobbie Be Good*.

"Here," she said. "For you, Mr. Karaoke Band Man." She handed him the case.

"My name is Corey." He took the case, briefly looking at the low resolution cover. Bobbie's pixelated smile grinned back at him, He was amazed at what computers could do today.

"I know, but everybody at karaoke has a karaoke name, and Corey is a boring name."

"Corey isn't a boring name!" he protested. "You don't find my name to be all rock n' roll?"

"Nope. I don't know you from your band. I know you from karaoke."

"Then Karaoke Band Man is my name," Corey conceded as he slipped the case into the inner pocket of his jean jacket. The singing clerk handed him his change.

"Let me know what you think of it."

"I will."

"Bye-bye, Mr. Karaoke Band Man."

"See you later, Bobbie Be Good. Time for me to get back on my Taun-Taun and look for Commander Skywalker," he said with a deadpan delivery. She let loose a nervous laugh in acknowledgment. Corey wasn't sure she got the *Star Wars* reference.

He pulled his jean jacket tight against the hooded sweatshirt underneath, inhaled the stale air of the convenience store and shivered, anticipating the return to the elements awaiting outside. The longer he thought about it, the deeper the snow was getting. He pushed through the glass and aluminum door, back into the storm.

•

At least another inch had fallen while he'd been in the store. The sun was starting to go down, too. Despite being left running, the car's windows were covered in a half inch of fresh snow. He wiped off the windows with his sleeve before pumping the gas. By the time he finished filling up, the windows were covered again.

Better judgment prompted Corey to use the station's window cleaner squeegee to brush the car off before driving away. He climbed in and popped Bobbie's CD in the car's player. She opened with a respectable version of Patsy Cline's "Crazy".

Not bad, he thought. *A lot better than what I heard last night.*

He put the car in drive and drove off, away from the gas station. As it turned out, Bobbie Be Good's tracks were good listening for cruising around in snowstorms. It was the only thing working in his favor. As soon as he pulled out of the lot, the road failed to let him get any traction.

"Don't do this to me, you motherfucker!" He spun the wheel at the perfect angle, caught something less ice covered and propelled the car forward, albeit slowly. Patsy Cline's lyrics serenaded him for two minutes of constant spinning and sliding. It segued into Bobbie's take on Bonnie Tyler, and the epic Steinman penned "Total Eclipse of the Heart". As the song played in all its majesty, it dawned on him that only two kinds of vehicles were going to pass these roads and make it home tonight: snow plows or snowmobiles, and nothing in between.

He was stuck in Fenton until this shit storm was over.

"Fuck! Fuck! Fuck!" He pounded his fists on the dashboard. Well, at least he had someplace he could go back to. He forced the car down the road, back to Bella's house. He was more than certain she would let him back in. He turned onto Park street to find it was impassable. *Fuck!* Corey recognized he should have stayed put all along.

The Key Bank on the corner of Park and Main sat kitty-corner from Corey's fishtailing Cavalier. Bobbie broke into Pat Benatar's "Heartbreaker" as the CD started to skip and repeat.

What's this, the rap version? It was certainly something different. Unfortunately, it didn't do anything for the song. Corey ejected the CD. *So much for Bobbie Be Good's cheap demo disc.*

In silence, Corey managed to get the Chevy into the bank's mostly plowed parking lot and under the drive-thru bay. It was a short walk through the snow to Bella's place from there, if it were indeed where he would go. The car's tires squealed as they grabbed pure tarmac for the first time this day.

Corey sat in the car for an eternity, gaining the gumption to make the hike up the road to Bella's. He tried playing Bobbie's CD from the beginning, but none of it would play now.

He was in no rush to hear those voices again, but the sex with Bella was excellent. He could see her house through the gray twilight. What would she say? What would he say to her? Would she even let him back in? He sucked in his pride and set forth through the snow. He prayed to God the voices wouldn't be there when he returned. He hoped they were a result of his over drinking and subsequent hangover.

CHAPTER 4

**SATURDAY, DECEMBER 16TH, 1989 9:40AM
FRENCHMAN'S BAY, LAKE ONEIDA,
MADISON COUNTY, NY
LAKE EFFECT SNOW ACCUMULATION: 16"**

Another lake effect storm, blowing off Lake Ontario, had struck. It was a wide band of snow, covering the real estate between the port cities of Oswego and Fenton, and stretching out across Syracuse, then over Oneida Lake. The snow band was so thick visibility was next to nothing once you entered its path.

The storm blanketed Central New York in more than a foot of snow, and in doing so, created an outdoors man's wet dream of white powder as far east of the Great Lake as the city of Utica, some sixty miles away. In between the rural countryside bordering Lake Ontario, Syracuse, and Utica was the Mohawk River Valley and the aforementioned Lake Oneida. Surrounded by summer cottages, marinas, and farmland, the large inland lake was the local ice fisherman's go-to. During a storm of this magnitude, the conditions were perfect for catching fish. Or so Scott Cooper thought.

Scoop, as his friends and just about anybody else called him, used the storm as an excuse to go ice fishing on a Sunday morning. He sat on a metal folding chair in his fishing hut, bundled up in a flannel winter jacket and winter overalls. The outfit was completed with thick gloves, a plaid scarf and black snowmobiler's boots. An Arctic Cat El Tigre 6000 snowmobile sat outside the hut, snow covering its sleek frame.

Inside the hut, a kerosene heater on high kept the shelter warm and toasty as the elements piled snow outside. Ice fishing was Scoop's time to think. He loved fishing any time of the year. Trout in spring, bass in summer, perch and walleye in winter.

The temperature had risen high enough within the hut to motivate Scoop to take his hat off. His mop of brown hair fell out as a result, falling across his eyes and beard. At only twenty-two years old, Scott was on his way to possessing a ZZ Top beard and a matching head of hair. He'd had the beard growing since high school, and it now came down to his chest. He was starting to find the humor in his arrest and release by the Madison County Sheriffs at his junior prom, six years ago. It wasn't every day you saw a high school student standing six feet tall with a full beard, so he couldn't actually blame the cops for thinking he was lying and not kidnapping a prom queen. It was something to laugh about while drinking at the bar, he supposed, despite making dating through his senior year nearly impossible.

Scoop loved music. At night and on weekends, he would DJ at one of the local titty bars, spinning everything from Anthrax to Duran Duran, or perform in his cover band, Scene of the Crime. He played rhythm guitar and sang a little, mostly KISS or Tom Petty if he did. Regardless of which he participated in, the end result was always loud.

In the hut, fishing, there was no music. The absolute epitome of boring, and Scoop loved every tedious minute of it. Sometimes you needed it, the quiet, the down time. Today was no different from any other time. It was peaceful. Uneventful, and except for the white noise of the blowing wind and occasional fish ringing the line bell, it was silent.

Until this morning.

Until now.

The wind outside the shelter picked up speed. It blew at the canvas, whipping into the fabric, creating a rhythmic pattern. It reminded Scoop of "Jailbait" from Motorhead, one of his favorite songs to play with the band. He hummed the melody, and sure enough, it fit.

"Well, ain't that a hoot?" he said aloud before humming along with the pattern, adding, "We are Motorhead, and we play rock 'n roll!" He made the devil horn sign with both hands and banged his head.

A pungent stench rode upon the blowing wind and seeped through the fabric, assaulting Scoop's nose. He could taste it on the air: a reeking, fetid, noxious odor. He first wondered how enough fish to create a stink of this magnitude could spoil in freezing temperatures.

And then he heard the ice cracking underneath him.

This isn't happening, he thought, *the ice has got to be a foot or more thick right now.*

But crack it did, in spite of the thickness.

Scoop felt his nape hairs rise, not from the cold cutting into the hut, but from fear. Uncomfortable, Scoop shifted in his seat. The metal frame of the chair creaked a chorus in unison with the crackling of the frozen lake. The kerosene heater rattled and popped up off the plywood sheet it rested upon, the metal and glass surrounding the wick clanging together when it landed.

Everything went silent, except for the wind. The stench lingered in the frozen air. Scoop held his breath, afraid to exhale. A few more moments passed until he finally released and drew in another breath.

An air bubble popped out of the sixteen-inch diameter opening Scoop's fishing lines hung into. It was followed by a second, and then more, until a boiling froth issued forth, splashing the interior. Water hissed as it bounced off the kerosene heater. Scoop stared in disbelief as the liquid sprayed his face. Each drop felt like a dagger of ice as it struck his forehead and cheeks.

This isn't happening, he thought, *how could this be happening?*

"What the fuck?"

A geyser of near freezing water erupted from the hole in the ice, blowing the hut's frame and fabric into the snowy air. Scoop now found himself exposed to the elements. Snowflakes popped and crackled on the kerosene heater. He heard a fluttering sound in the distance, turned his head toward it, and saw nothing but falling flakes of snow.

Something wet slapped on the ice surrounding the hole. Scoop saw a day glow blue tentacle, squirming about, toothed suction cups pulsing. The emergence of a second tentacle was all it took to break Scoop from staring and prompt him to action.

"Fuck this shit, ain't no fuckin' octopuses in Oneida fucking Lake!" He pulled his hat back over his head and slipped his gloves back on before standing up and taking a couple of short steps to his snowmobile. Scoop didn't bother wiping the snow off the sled. He hopped on the long seat and flicked the machine on. The Arctic Cat's 500cc liquid cooled Suzuki engine roared to life. He felt the machine's horsepower jerk him in place as it sped off in a straight line toward the shore. He liked his vehicles to be fast. Nothing on the snow had more power than an El Tigre.

The roar of the engine hid the clamor of the line of exploding ice and snow flying into the air behind him. Something was burrowing through the lake ice in pursuit, and though Scoop couldn't hear it, he could *sense* the danger. The El Tigre 6000 was the fastest snowmobile ever built, or so the ads declared. It hit eighty-five miles an hour in a matter of seconds. Whatever was following Scoop was matching the machine in speed. He opened the clutch and felt the power of the engine as the four-hundred- seventy-five-pound machine cut through the snow.

The storm's wind had created a whiteout, obscuring a flotsam pile sitting on the lakefront. Scott Cooper and his El Tigre 6000 snowmobile slammed into the debris at full speed. A magnificent plume of powder and timber billowed into the falling snow. The sled came to an abrupt halt, bending both front skis in half as it flipped forward. The momentum catapulted the driver into the air. Scoop found himself tumbling onto the shoreline, driving him into the snowpack. He lay dazed, buried in the snow, unable to move, his body tingling from the neck down.

"Son of a bitch!" he cursed. He found it hard to breathe, a great pressure on his chest prevented him from inhaling. The impact had temporarily paralyzed him from the neck down. He tried not to panic; if he was lucky, he'd recover soon, then he could make his way up to Route 31 where he would certainly find a residence and shelter.

Jailbait, baby!

Scoop thought the disembodied voice sounded sexy until he felt his body being pulled back toward the lake. He was dragged through snow, grass and ice, and briefly heard the still grumbling motor of his snowmobile. This lasted only a moment before he found himself immersed in the frigid waters of the lake. Feeling returned to his body, the tingling replaced by a burning cold. A single gasp for air filled his lungs with frigid lake water. And then he felt nothing at all.

•

SATURDAY, MARCH 13, 1993 4:17 P.M.
305 PARK ST., FENTON, NY
SNOWFALL: 14"

Corey was still soaked up to the knees, even more when he reached her stoop. He could hear something playing, Pantera maybe? He wasn't sure. He pressed the doorbell and once it chimed, the music volume diminished. He heard footsteps and the tumblers turning from a deadbolt. The door opened and heat from inside the house rushed out to him.

"Back so soon?" Bella said, smiling. She stood before him, as magnificent as she had been at the bar last night, still in the little black nightie he had left her in.

"Well, yeah. Either my tires suck ass or the roads are impassable. Or a combination of the two," he answered.

"What about Mr. Whiskers?"

"Who?" Corey was drawing a blank.

"Your cat?"

Oh shit! He mentally backpedaled. She was good. Without blinking an eye, Corey carried on the lie, "Oh, I guess he'll be hungry when I get home tomorrow."

"I'm sure he will be. I guess you want to come back in?"

"I'd like to, if you don't mind."

"Well, you did shovel my driveway out earlier, the least I can do is give you shelter," a devilish grin appeared on her face, "and I'm sure you have other ways of paying room and board." Corey felt his cock stir to life as the words dripped off her lips. One thing he couldn't argue, she was a fantastic fuck.

"I'm sure we can come to some arrangement." She pushed the door wide open, grabbed him by the collar and pulled him into her arms. The door shut behind him in the wake of activity and she kissed him, her tongue invading his mouth. It seemed to caress his soul.

"Let's go to bed," she breathed. "I need your cock inside me."

Corey shrugged. "Why the hell not?"

I knew you'd be back.

"You did, ha?"

I did.

She held him by the hand and led him away from her living room to her place of pleasure.

"... hello ..."

Corey didn't hear *Their* voice welcome him back. If he had, he may have taken his chances with the weather.

She pulled his clothing off and the sex marathon continued, unabated, as if Corey had never left Bella's house.

●

The fucking snow continued to fall with accumulations previously unseen in a twelve-hour time period. Over a foot of it dumped on Central New York, and the storm wasn't ending anytime soon. Blizzard conditions held most of the East Coast under an icy death grip. Thunder, snow and lightning could be seen and heard, the *Hadiwennoda:dye's* spirits of Onondaga folklore at play, Corey thought. It was truly remarkable to experience, and Corey did so, from inside the warmth of Bella's home and her bed. And her sex.

Bella appeared to love every water-soaked flake drifting out of the massive storm as much as she loved being sodomized. Corey had her bent over the side of the bed, at her request, of course. He wasn't normally an anal guy, but Bella begged him to tap her in the brown eye, so he did. It had already driven her to a half dozen squirting orgasms, and the taboo act turned him to steel with each thrust. His member was numb from use over the past day. He wouldn't be coming any time soon, much to Bella's delight and Corey's distress. He needed a rest, but this girl did not want to stop. Finally, when he felt his legs start to give out and he could take it no longer, Corey pushed hard into Bella's rectum and arched his back, faking an orgasm.

If girls can do it I can, Corey thought to himself. It wasn't the first time he'd ended a marathon sex session with a fake nut. Maybe someday he would pass this advice down to his own son, as his father had offered when least needed.

The younger Collins collapsed at his lover's side, spent from a day of shoveling snow and sex. If the worst thing he would deal with was more sex, Corey could live with it, but he needed to sleep. He hadn't heard a single errant voice come whisper from the shadows since he arrived.

He drifted off with no nightmares, no voices. There was nothing. His mind, knowing full well what would await it, chose not to dream this night. In his slumber, Corey was unaware the Nor'easter had only completed the first of three acts in an all-natural production which would continue for at least another twelve hours. By this time, approximately twenty-seven million tons would fall, nearly 13 cubic miles of snow, across the East Coast.

•

SUNDAY, JANUARY 19TH 1992, 10:54PM
FENTON HOTEL, FENTON, NY
LAKE EFFECT SNOWFALL TOTAL: 16"

Patrick Hallenbeck, the stage name chosen by Pat Stephenson, wanted to thank the bar for outnumbering "them" tonight, but he couldn't. The "them" in question were Pat and his guitar, a beater dreadnought with an anegre finish and a big sticker declaring "SHAMROCKS." If you counted the bartender and cook, it was a tie. The first night of his East Coast stand up tour transformed into a dress rehearsal, thanks to the wonderful weather of Fenton and the college's holiday semester break. Lake effect snow had been falling since Tuesday, and just over a foot of it had accumulated, to be precise. As a result, nobody was out on a Saturday night.

"Mac, how do you know you're from fecking Central New York?" He asked the bartender, utilizing the charming, yet faux, Irish accent he incorporated into his comedy routine.

"Wait five minutes, and the weather will change, ya know?" the bartender replied.

"You bet your ass, not only will it change, that shit will get worse, laddy. *Slainte!*" Pat toasted in Gaelic, slammed his beer, slapped two dollars on the bar and zipped up his leather jacket.

"How far you got to go?"

"Not far. Staying at my mate's trailer in Criminal Estates." The bartender chuckled at the name bestowed upon Casual Estates, Fenton's white trash trailer park on the outskirts of the small city. Pat slipped a ski hat with a fuzzy ball on his balding head. Only three years out of high school, just old enough to legally drink, and he had developed what he called the *yarmulke* scar in his red mop of hair.

"Well good luck out there. Where are you playing next?"

"I'm in Rochester tomorrow night, Buffalo on Monday, then Niagara Falls on Wednesday, Thursday and Friday. Hopefully it will work out better than tonight."

"I think you should be good. Especially in the Falls."

"If I have enough gas money to make it there, lad."

"Hey, I'm sorry, I gotta make money, too. I can't pay you what isn't in the drawer."

"It is what it is, Mac." He marched off, guitar in hand, to the door and the weather outside. "Peace out, Mr. Mac Dixie."

"Peace!" The comedian heard the bar owner reply as the door shut on a hydraulic hinge behind him. Pat nearly froze in place when the twenty-two-degree air hit his lungs. He trudged through the snow to his car, a blue Chevette, parked in front of the bar. The subcompact was buried under a fresh coating of snow. At least two, maybe three inches had fallen since he arrived at the bar earlier in the evening. He wiped it off with his free arm, unlocked the door and tossed his guitar in the back seat. He ran an arm over each window on the driver's and passenger's sides of the small car, streaking the snow off. Moments later, he was in the bucket seat, ignition turned and heat blowing on the window, defrosting the glass. He let it idle for a few minutes as the engine warmed and heated the car's interior. One advantage of a small car was it didn't take long to heat up.

He ignored the car's seat belt alarm; he never wore it, and the bell would stop soon as he got going. Pat put the car in drive and slowly pulled out of the parking lot. His tires crunched the fresh snow coating the ground. The road was slick, but manageable. He recently had snow tires put on the car in anticipation of inclement weather on the tour. He found himself on nearby Route 104 in good time, cruising along just under the speed limit, erring on the side of caution.

He got lost in thought, thinking about his family. Pat played off being a full-blooded mick, coming straight off the boat. As far as his mother was concerned, this was true within a generation. But the truth was his father fucked Germany into the bloodline with Pat and his siblings.

Patrick turned on the cassette player. The Scream's biggest hit, "Critical Mass", blasted out of the speakers. Until recently they were the biggest thing, but the now infamous fire at the stadium killed the band and all those people. Their singer was a hot Asian chick, no pun intended, considering the aftermath. What was her name? Kara? Tara? He couldn't remember.

Then the music went sour, slowing down and speeding up, warbling. The tape became garbled, then started changing from side to side, the mechanism within clicking over and over.

"Fuck!" Pat lost the manufactured Irish accent in the stress of it all. He ejected the cassette from the player. Tape trailed behind the cassette.

"God fucking dammit!" He threw the cassette and mangled tape on the passenger's seat. So much for the Scream.

He saw the shape walking down the highway ahead of him almost too late. At first a dark splotch in the snow shower, Pat soon realized, no, *he knew*, it was a woman. She was dressed in black, which had made seeing her in the snowfall more difficult. Then he heard something slap the rear panel of the car, and he was sure he'd hit her.

"Son of a bitch!" Pat shouted, pulled over and stopped the car. How much had he drunk tonight? Two, three beers? Maybe a couple of shots. He couldn't be drunk, could he? Regardless, if he hit a person, he couldn't let them die on the side of the road in a snowstorm.

He slammed the vehicle into park and jumped out. The red brake lights of his car fading from site as he ran down the road. He got to the spot where he was sure he'd hit her.

Nobody was there, only falling snow.

Had he imagined it? He couldn't have. She had been there, he knew it, dressed in black, walking on the road side. He knew— no, *he felt*—she had black hair and green eyes. The woman had been standing right fucking here on the side of the road. The snow continued to fall and stick to him and everything else.

Pat walked in a semi-circle off the road's shoulder, stopping on occasion to twist and turn, looking for the woman. An acrid stench assaulted him, overpowering the exhaust of his nearby, still running car. Eye watering and revolting, he wondered if a skunk had been startled nearby. Then he heard somebody speak to him. Or at least he thought he did.

Come to Mommy, baby.

"Mommy?" He said. Pat turned his head to where he thought he heard the voice come from, *but it's coming from everywhere!* His subconscious told him. Even more concerning, no one was there. Who was talking to him?

"Hello? Where are you? Are you hurt?" He called. He heard nothing but blowing wind and the idling engine of the Chevette. He called out again, with no results. Losing his voice and tired of the stench, he decided to return to the car.

He took two steps and stopped, watching the red lights on the rear of his Chevette levitate into the snowy air. Snow and ice fell from the car's undercarriage. Something held it aloft.

"You've got to be fucking kidding me!" He heard metal creak, then the car launched into the air, away from the highway, into the wooded lot hugging the road. Pat tore his felt hat off, threw it to the ground and kicked it. "No, cocksucker, no! This can't be motherfucking happening!"

Pat fell. He felt his face slam into an exposed block of tarmac on the road's shoulder before the pressure of whatever had clamped onto his ankles registered with his brain. Dazed, bolts of pain shooting up from his smashed nose, he made a weak attempt to push himself back up. His hands slipped in the snow, and he cracked his forehead on a block of ice, splitting open his forehead and sending his brain spinning in a vortex of pain.

I'm your Mommy!

Blood poured from the wound on his temple. The sensation of warmth on his face was in stark contrast to the snow sliding up his back, under his jacket and t-shirt, as he was dragged away from the road in the snow by his feet. It took a few moments, but he came to his senses and realized something was pulling him off the road into the snow. He flailed his arms about, trying to grab hold of something, anything. His body swayed to the left and right in his attempts to break free of whatever had hold of him. His midsection slammed into a tree, and he heard a loud snap from inside his body. He wasn't sure what it was, a rib, maybe two, perhaps? Or maybe not a rib at all?

Then it came to him, the clarity of mind brought on by having your sternum crushed on a pine tree. Tara, *yes Tara was her name,* the singer of the doomed band. Taking a titular cue, he came to the summation there was nothing he could do. Except...

...scream.

CHAPTER 5

SUNDAY, MARCH 14, 1993 12:09 A.M.
305 PARK ST. FENTON, NY
SNOWFALL: 20"

Corey woke, his mind in a fog. He was alone in the bed, his legs cold from laying in the rather large wet spot left behind from the lovemaking marathon. He had a *Groundhog Day* moment, recalling he had woken up in much the same manner once already. Only then he was greeted with the scent of cooking bacon, and this time he wasn't so lucky. This time all he felt a desire to do was piss.

The voices still hadn't made an appearance. The only other constant was the snow, still falling at an alarming rate.

Not bothering to dress, he hopped out of the bed and made his way to the bathroom. The house was surprisingly silent and dark. He saw the snow falling through the bay window in the living room. Frost had started to build on the inside of the window. Corey was shocked that the conditions were worsening, something he hadn't believed possible.

Motherfucker, this is exactly what they said it would be!

"Bella?" He called. She didn't answer. He found the bathroom and pissed, taking care to leave the door open as he did. Still no ethereal voices greeted him. Corey was becoming more comfortable with the situation now. He surely had been hallucinating earlier, much to his relief. His belly grumbled.

Warrior needs food badly, his internal jokester quipped, drawing forth a laugh. He stepped into the kitchen, opened the fridge door to find something to eat.

It was empty.

Not a goddamn thing was in the fridge. It didn't look as if any food had been stored in the unit, ever. It was factory clean, with yellowed packing tape still lining the interior. It smelled musty, and didn't appear to have ever been plugged in. *Where did she make breakfast from?* Maybe she had a bigger fridge in the garage.

"The fuck...? Bella? Where are you?" Corey closed the refrigerator and looked outside the kitchen window. The driveway was filled with snow. All the work Corey had done earlier in the day had been erased. He noticed lights from the garage shining through the windows of the bay door onto the driveway.

Corey opened the door leading from the house to the garage and was greeted with an unexpected spectacle. A beat up, baby blue Chevy Chevette sat in the back of the garage, four flat tires and a shattered windshield. The car was in rough shape.

Even weirder, standing before him, was a complete stage set up for a band, from instruments to lighting. A drum kit with a double Nordic Bjork rune emblazoned on the bass head sat in the back on a high riser. Bent microphone stands were placed strategically on the stage for two backup singers. A lone, wireless mic on an aluminum stand stood in the center. Corey was certain the middle mic was for a vocalist, a coincidence he found all too convenient, considering he was a lead singer. Facing the stage, suspended above the door, was a large screen television.

"Are you fucking kidding me?" he said out loud.

"I told you I had a karaoke machine." Bella stepped out from behind the stage. She was still wearing the same black cotton and lace nightie, except she complimented it with the denim vest she wore at the bar. She looked as alluring now as she had all weekend. He fought the urge to take her on the stage. His cock ached, and he remembered he was nude as it stiffened. He covered his genitals with a free hand and pointed to the stage with his other.

"This is a bit more extensive than a karaoke machine, Bella. This is top of the line stuff. Marshall stacks." He pointed at the drums. "Tamas, and those lights aren't cheap. Where did you get all of this shit?"

"Well, babe, I also told you I had an opening in my personal band for a new singer, if you recall."

"Yeah, but I didn't think it would be this!"

"What else would it be?" She walked over to him, exposing as much leg as possible during the process. Bella copied Corey and covered her vagina with one hand. As she got closer to him, he saw she was doing more than covering it up, she was masturbating. How could he say no to this?

"Sing for me, Corey. Please?" She gestured to the stage with her free hand while diddling herself with the other. He climbed the stairs to the stage, and she followed. He'd never been on stage in the buff before. No sooner did he get to the top step, he heard Bon Jovi's "Wanted: Dead or Alive" start to play over the speakers. The overhead monitor counted down, indicating when the vocals would start. He stepped up to the microphone, and Bella stepped in front of him. They stared at each other for a moment, then Bella dropped to her knees. Corey gasped as she licked and tickled his cock with her tongue, then engulfed him with her mouth. This made two firsts today. He'd never had sex on stage before, either.

Corey grabbed the microphone and focused on the lyrics on the screen, not on the fellatio. He sang the song, adding a bluesy, earthy feel to the melody. All the while Bella hungrily performed oral on him, never once removing his cock from her mouth. By the time the guitar solo ended, he was close to climaxing. She didn't release him until Corey proclaimed he'd been everywhere and rocked them all. She milked him for the last minute of the song. Much to his surprise, he remained stiff the whole time. Another first in a long list of firsts. Bella was a miracle worker.

The music stopped, and the garage went silent.

"Oh baby, I think you have a job," Bella told Corey as she licked a little of him off her lip, "I think … you … do." She stretched the words out long and seductive and traced a finger up his torso.

"Oh yeah? But I'm already in a band."

"I know. Can't a girl dream? Shut up and fuck me some more. That's your job, baby." She turned around, bent over and sat back on Corey's rock-hard cock. This made a third *first* for the day. He'd never maintained an erection this long before, especially after blowing a load. He felt her warmth embrace him, and all thoughts of how and why and where left his mind.

Bella broke away from their coitus, turned around and pushed Corey down to his knees in front of her. She hiked her nightie up, exposing her steaming hot, dripping sex.

"Lick me, please," she half asked, half commanded. So he did. She held his face in place, not letting him move. He didn't care. He didn't want to stop. It gave his sore cock a break. He performed vigorously for her until his jaw was sore, and he couldn't move it any more.

Somewhere in the garage, a door on squeaky hinges opened. Corey tried to turn his head toward the sound, but she continued to hold him in place, preventing any movement not requiring oral pleasure of her. He could feel her hands running down his back.

"Keep licking me. Please, don't stop," Bella begged. Corey obliged by picking up the pace. He was in the middle of spelling the alphabet out on the tip of her clitoris for a third time when heard a double tap on the high hat of the drum kit behind him.

Is somebody watching us? Corey wondered. The hiss of a tube amp firing up followed to his right. *Somebody is in here with us!* He was sure of it. *What was going on?* He fought to escape her clutches, but she wouldn't let him move. He heard a single E note ring out on a bass guitar. It resonated in the air. An A pentatonic guitar scale sealed the deal. He pushed back with all his might and broke free of Bella's icy grasp. Corey fell on his back on the stage. A stench assaulted his nose, overcoming her aroma, reminding him of a filthy lavatory.

Reminding him of Bella's unclean toilet.

"What the fuck?" He looked to his left and his right. Standing to either side of them was a person … mostly. What remained of their decaying bodies were holding a guitar and bass, respectively. They were both in an advanced state of desiccation, their skin taught from a lack of moisture and drawn tight over the skull. Full mops of hair adorned their heads, but Corey could tell they were wigs. For a moment he thought he was surrounded by clones of Iron Maiden's mascot, Eddie the Head. Then he looked at them closely. He *knew* them from somewhere.

"What the fuck is going on here?" Corey demanded.

The musicians remained silent, holding their instruments and waiting for their cue. Bella was also without words. She crouched before Corey, ready to pounce. She had a white nightie on now, he noted, and wondered when she had time for the wardrobe change.

The weirdest thing, though, was the trip he was on. Bella kept shifting, coming in and out of focus. One blink of an eye beheld her nearly on top of him again, then the next she was at the far edge of the stage. Corey couldn't do anything, couldn't move. Then he heard *Their* goddamned voice again, clearer and closer than he'd ever heard it before.

"*Sing for US! Sing for HER!*"

Corey felt fright race through his being as he lay there, helpless. At any moment she could be on top of him again. The thought of any further contact with whatever she was made his skin clammy. Instead she moved backwards, extending her body and slinking off the stage on her belly feet first, her crystal blue eyes still focused on Corey's.

Her eyes …

As she moved, he found he could move, too. He followed her, to the edge of the stage, then off and forward into her embrace. The instruments behind him came to life.

Her …

He heard the familiar chords of Pink Floyd's epic "Set Your Controls for the Heart of the Sun". It droned on, the perfect psychedelic soundtrack for a mind fuck.

Eyes …

Mind fuck, Corey laughed. What an appropriate assertion of the situation! He'd spent much of the last 24 hours fucking her, now he figured it was time to flip the tables. Bella's opportunity to get out the strap-on and give Corey a mental pegging.

Her eyes!

They were deep and eternal. Corey Collins, lead singer of the band Well of Sorrow, felt his mind falling into the madness in the depths of Bella's eyes.

•

THEN...

Awoken by the incredible temperature, the seed of Sbli'rldlnisa-aea—the Great Old Goddess of the Ice and Snow—fell from the sky to the Earth. Encased in a shell of stone, the seed burned cherry red, flames roaring as it cascaded through the atmosphere before finally crashing into snow, ice, and rock. Inside the seed's walls, Sbli'rldlnisa-aea grew.

There she sat, buried in an unassuming grave. Covered by granite and bedrock, snow and ice, hungry and trapped for eons, she waited to be freed. The snows, attracted to her being, piled high upon her glacial prison, moving back and forth across the surface of the earth, scarring it and shaping the land throughout the millennia.

Sbli'rldlnisa-aea knew nothing, only her name and the hunger, and though she could feel sustenance around her, she could not feed. Sbli'rldlnisa-aea yet remained a prisoner, until the day when the earth shifted, the ice fell and extricated her.

Finally liberated, Sbli'rldlnisa-aea swam free, through the snow and ice, searching for the food she had felt before. The prey, as it turned out, wasn't as willing to sustain her as other forms of nutrition had been in the past. No, this prey fought back, making it impossible for her to eat, to get stronger. She gained another name, Angraboda. The prey believed she was the mother of Hel and Fenris. Sbli'rldlnisa-aea never did anything to change the belief.

The prey was smart; it lived away from the snow, making any attempt to feed a risky endeavor. Outside of snow she was weaker than her prey, vulnerable. She couldn't feed en masse, to do so would be folly. Instead, she would need to lure the prey away.

Starving and fearing she would be unable to defend her being against the threats this world provided, Sbli'rldlnisa-aea cried. While she hid in waiting, singing her mournful song, she finally learned a use for her pain and exploited it.

A traveler, upon hearing the entrancing melody and unaware of what she was, passed too close. She struck him unaware, wrapping her tail about him, squeezing the life from his bones as she secreted digestive juices, melting her prey as she absorbed him into her being. In this moment Sbli'rldlnisa-aea became more than she had been, and so did her hapless victim. She felt the power racing through her being as she fed. When she had finished absorbing the nutrients from his body, she expelled the rest, defecating an oily, black ooze from the pores of her skin. This viscous byproduct was living and as eternal as she in essence. It followed her, wishing only to satisfy Sbli'rldlnisa-aea and only wanting to hear her beautiful song in return. Only then would it be satisfied. Thus, The First, as what was left of her victim went on to be called, sang for her. Hoping it would release her.

"Sbli'rldlnisa-aea, Gudinnen av alle ting."

… The goddess of all things …

"Sbli'rldlnisa-aea For himmelens droning."

The First cried in love and devotion of his goddess. She had no choice but to reply, a baleful song lamenting her love. It was glorious to behold. Through their symbiotic bond, The First taught Sbli'rldlnisa-aea much about her prey in his desire to satisfy her. Humans, as she learned her prey called themselves, were a fickle lot, but easy to manipulate, and easier to seduce. She found she could take the form of whatever prey she consumed and used these to satiate her hunger.

With each meal Sbli'rldlnisa-aea became stronger, and as she grew stronger, so too did the storms. The lands she ruled were a desert of snow and ice, becoming home to the hardiest of creatures brave enough to endure the elements. Caribou, bears, foxes, penguins, hares, and their ilk thrived under Sbli'rldlnisa-aea's watchful eye. She could have fed on them, but it was the things inside her prey's heads which made them a delicacy. All animals living in harmony with the landscape she had created, all prey of her prey. If she couldn't go to her food source, she would bring her food source to her. This symbiotic relationship lasted for centuries. They thought her a goddess. She was Angraboda!

Until her prey had enough of their goddess.

The humans learned how to fight back against her, avoiding her lands when they felt she would be present, creating armor and *weapons to fight her away. The prey forced the hunter to adapt. Sbli'rldlnisa-aea liked to lure her prey while in the skin of the opposite sex. She enjoyed copulating with them, slowly feeding off them as she did, little by little, slowly taking away parts of their essence. She found if she could maintain a stocked herd of prey, all under her control, she could limit her need to interact with her prey. Hunt and eat at her leisure.*

Until the prey caught on.

The winter had been small. A warmer than normal spring brought with it the early removal of the snowpack from the hills surrounding Sbli'rldlnisa-aea's den, leaving her with nowhere to run when they came. She held onto her human form; it was easier to blend in with the prey if she managed to escape.

She woke one sunny morning to the sound of drums, a tribal pattern pounding an entrancing rhythm. It resonated through the walls of her dark cave, soothing her, calming her, making it difficult for her to hold form. She ran to the drums, conjuring all the power she could to bring forth the weather she could thrive in. The freak spring storm she created buried her aggressors under a blanket of snow, giving her the opening she needed to strike. She let her human form slip away and dove into the fresh powder, intent on causing harm to the prey. How dare they assault her; how dare they attack the sanctity of Sbli'rldlnisa-aea! The humans would pay for this. She swam through the snow, eliminating each drummer in sequence and after she had ended the last of them, the storm stopped.

Unsure of why it had, Sbli'rldlnisa-aea realized too late she had fallen into a trap. She watched as gelded human warriors, each covered in armor with an eye plucked out and their ears burned off, appeared from the wood line. Hidden underneath brush, away from Sbli'rldlnisa-aea's sensitive ears, they had waited long hours for the opportunity to strike.

The determined warriors split into two groups. As one proceeded to purify the contents of her lair with fire, the others trapped her, blocking the entrance to her lair. Sbli'rldlnisa-aea could hear The First and The Many Who Followed scream in agony as they met the final death.

The warriors then surrounded her, netted her, and dragged her into a lead-lined casket. The box was sealed with molten iron. Trapped within its confines, Sbli'rldlnisa-aea was blind, deaf, mute, and alone.

•

Corey couldn't handle the vision anymore. His body quivered from palpitations as he violently shook his head until he *un-saw* all of it. Bella stood before him, watching him move, her head cocked to the side.

"What the fuck are you?" Corey asked her. Her answer wasn't audible. He heard in his head.

Bella. I'm Bella, your goddess of metal.

"The fuck you are!" Corey replied to her psychic response.

Sing for me, Corey.

"*Sing for Us! Sing for Us! Sing for Us!*" the ghastly zombie-musicians chanted in a Gregorian style.

This was madness. Corey tried to rationalize the situation. This shit didn't happen. Girls you picked up at a bar were crazy, yes. They might chop your dick off while you're sleeping, yes. They care not life sucking, zombie making, out of this fucking world aliens! Aliens aren't real!

Corey, always proud of his quick thinking, saw an opportunity to run into her house and took it. He sprinted past Bella and found the door into the kitchen was unlocked.

You can't escape, lover. She was in his head again.

"The fuck I can't," he said and slammed the door behind him. Corey turned the deadbolt and attached the chain. The door opened out, so a barricade would be useless. He wasn't sure how long the locks would hold. He ran to the bedroom and wasted no time getting dressed. He could hear something weakly pounding on the door. It was the musicians, chanting their mantra over and over.

"*… sing for us … sing … for … US!*"

The sound was muffled by the door, something Corey was grateful for. His socks were still wet from the day before. He opened her dresser to find all the clothes were for men.

Just when you thought this couldn't get any weirder. He dug through them, found a pair of roughly matching socks, a toque with a red fuzzy ball on top, and a pair of snowmobiling gloves. He'd be ready for the weather this time.

The pounding on the door to the garage continued, echoing through the house, as did the voices both in and outside of Corey's head.

Lover, don't leave. Where would you go?

"*... US ... you ... are ... US ...*"

Corey tried not to focus on Bella or the zombie dudes. He opened her closet to confirm a suspicion. It was full of men's shoes and boots. He shifted through them, found a matching pair of winter boots (the tongue even said Thinsulate®!) in his size, and he was off to the races, suiting up to run the fuck away from whatever the fuck Bella and the other guys were.

Corey, lover, open the door. Bella was in his head, someplace. He felt his groin stir at the thought of her.

"No! Fuck you!" Corey shook her out of his head, but the primal urge to copulate still lingered. His dick throbbed painfully in his jeans, restricted by the fabric. The banging on the door continued.

The zombies were useless, Corey concluded. No wonder Bella, or whatever she was, had been trapped for a millennia in a prison. She couldn't even open a garage door with the help of a pair of stooges.

Not the brightest of aliens, are you? Corey mentally taunted her, it, whatever, hoping the thing actually had a weird psychic power allowing it to hear the insult. He turned on the stereo and cranked the volume. Much to his surprise, Corey heard his band, Well of Sorrow, blast out of the speakers. It was their opening number, "Freakshow", and the driving rock song did a fantastic job of blocking the voices.

Circus coming to town,

Something wicked's come around.

Better run home turn on your lights!

The beast is running in the moonlight.

Corey heard himself sing about a werewolf on the prowl. It dawned on him he may not have met Bella by accident. Then the chorus of the song hit with the power of an arena rock anthem.

Ladies and gentlemen, boys and girls,

Glad you came to see the show!

The Freakshow, baby!

If she had their CD, then she knew who he was. She had led him here, and he had followed right along, a fly in a spider's web. In fact, Corey had been so foolish he had left and come back. Not again. He made sure his car keys were in his pocket and, for the second time today, ventured out into the storm.

CHAPTER 6

SUNDAY, MARCH 14, 1993 03:00 A.M.
305 PARK ST., FENTON, NY
SNOWFALL: 25"

Corey knew a foot of snow is one thing to behold, but dealing with it is another thing altogether. Walking through it is difficult, but the task can be managed. It's on par with walking through the shallows at a beach. You can drag your feet through it or raise each foot up and out of the depths. Either way, the end result is the same; it's inconvenient, slows you down some, and if you move too fast, it will trip you up.

Two feet of it is an entirely different story. Corey had discovered it's nearly fucking impossible.

Two feet of snow comes up to, or over, an average person's knees. Walking through this is a chore, to put it mildly. Lifting your legs in the manner required to move through snow quickly tires a person out. Trappers and hunters long ago found the best way to deal with deep snow was to stay on top of it. Snowshoes, designed to displace the snow and support the wearer, would be the desired foot attire at this moment in time for anyone unlucky enough to be walking around in it.

By the time Corey got to the end of the short driveway, he was ready to collapse from exhaustion. Each step was made harder by something internal pulling him back. He fought against it, fought against the snow. Each step brought fatigue and a feeling of dread and loneliness. The feeling of a broken heart. Corey knew a broken heart could turn to hateful anger at the flick of a switch. So he got angry and let the rage carry him away.

Corey wondered if it would ever stop snowing. If he could get to his car at the very least he'd be warm and relatively safe. He had filled the tank. The car could idle until morning, until the plows had done their job of clearing the way home.

He found the road was in a little better condition. Plows had come by on a regular pattern, making the road passable for emergency vehicles. Corey was optimistic he might be able to drive away tonight. He noted the further he got from the house, the less he felt it drawing him back. He was halfway down the block when he realized he hadn't heard the voices, hers or *Theirs* since he got out of the driveway and away from 305 Park Street. Whatever she was, whatever *They* were, he much preferred twenty-two degrees Fahrenheit and two feet of blowing snow.

Drifts as tall as six feet loomed about driveways and lots, obscuring the homes on Park Street and beyond. The banks on the sides of the road were twice as high, resembling a bobsled tunnel. Corey saw the single light of a snowmobile through the blowing white haze.

Be nice to have one of those right about now. His heart pounded in his chest from exertion. He stopped, bent over, panting. Steam and frost from his breath lingered in the air about his face. He looked up and saw the red of the traffic light at the corner. His destination wasn't far.

Time to move! He trudged through the snow, using all his remaining energy. The intersection of Main and Park became clearer. He could make out the structure of the bank and the drive-thru, and his car. It was still there, unmolested, not a drop of snow on it. The awning had effectively sheltered the vehicle. He dug out his car keys, unlocked the car and got in.

The seat was freezing, as was the interior, but it was dry and devoid of snow. He turned the car on and blew the heat at maximum. The CD player started up, playing Bobbie Be Good's interpretation of "Heart Breaker" uninterrupted and without skipping. It sounded pretty good, Corey noted. Within a few minutes the car's interior temperature had risen to a comfort level permitting Corey to remove his hat and gloves. He draped his hands on the steering wheel of the Cavalier. His breath steamed the window, then froze. He noted the icy fractals forming on the window as it cooled back down. They were hypnotizing, blending with the music as Bobbie Be Good moved into Heart's "All I Wanna Do Is Make Love to You." He fell asleep from exhaustion.

•

THEN...

Sbli'rldlnisa-aea slept, quietly mourning the loss of Them. Trapped inside the prison, she could do nothing else, for now. As she came to learn, the prisons of men last as long as their memories. Iron rusts and flakes away, and iron held the seal on her prison. When the last of it finally wasted away, she was too weak to open the stone coffin container. The restraints may have rusted off, but the rock had fused together. She was still trapped.

When Sbli'rldlnisa-aea heard the prey, after many decades, it made all thirteen of her hearts skip a beat. They reminded her aching belly of her hunger. She reached out and felt about for the first mind she could sing to. When she finally found one, he opened her prison shell, not knowing what he released on the world. She was sad to consume him—after all, he'd brought her freedom—but what better gift to bestow upon him other than to become The New First? She found the human prey in this new land much easier to feed on. They lacked the technology the others possessed, and thus lacked the weaponry to harm her. Their primitive weapons of bone, stone and wood were a far cry from the iron and steel she had grown accustomed to facing.

These people called her Ne-On-Yar-He, which translated in their language to the snow devil whore demon. Aware they couldn't harm *her, the prey soon learned to avoid her proximity. She discovered they were nomads for the most part, and she followed them.*

Sbli'rldlnisa-aea eventually found the perfect nesting spot, on the coast of a giant lake. Its location was a sweet spot for inclement weather she could manipulate in her favor. If she was smart, she could do this for an eternity. She had learned from her mistakes.

Centuries passed and nothing changed. Then she noticed prey, akin to those who had captured her, arriving with far deadlier weapons at their disposal. Tubes of steel firing projectiles replaced blades and armor. At first she helped the local prey in fighting off the invaders, and as a result she was briefly worshiped, again, as a goddess. She cared less for this. She fought against the invaders to defend her food stock.

Time passed, however briefly, and the trespassers became legion. And so she hid, knowing and fearing what they were capable of. Sbli'rldlnisa-aea preferred freedom. Even more so, she preferred to live. So she would hide. To hide from them, she would need to become them. She learned to blend in completely with her prey. She learned their language, she learned who to prey upon.

The philandering males were the easiest. They always came and were never missed when taken. Sbli'rldlnisa-aea would sing to them, luring the lusting fools to her lair where she would embrace her unsuspecting victims and add to Them. Jealous suitors of her victims often came seeking her for revenge. At first she readily dispatched them. It was only later she learned to maim and scar any of these scorned women coming for her. Letting them live kept the serious hunters away.

She found the times of war between factions of her prey to be fruitful. As eras changed and the land became more settled, so did her food supply. Her hunting grounds took her between a series of ports. She found plenty of sustenance through drifters and sailors.

As time passed and men became more civilized, the memory and fear of Sbli'rldlnisa-ae, of Angraboda, of Ne-On-Yar-He, disappeared, too. She had lost her goddess status, but she lived on.

The weather was perfect, most of the year. During the winter months she would gorge herself on prey, preparing for the lean summer and fall and the return of her beloved snow and ice. As time progressed, Sbli'rldlnisa-ae perfected the skill of preserving her victims and extending their usefulness, allowing her sustenance during the warmer months. They found it easy to control, manipulate, and animate the bodies. She continued to exist while They *got larger and larger.*

•

SUNDAY, MARCH 14, 1993 05:12 A.M.
KEY BANK, FENTON, NY
SNOWFALL: 31"

A thunderous pounding brought Corey out of his deep sleep. It was a fretful rest, his dreams focusing on the cosmic terror, its history unfolding before the screen of his mind's eye. The banging startled him back to reality. Corey bashed his knee on the steering column of the Cavalier, sending a jolt through the nerve in his leg. Steam obfuscated the window, hiding whoever was pounding. It was still dark, so he couldn't have been sleeping for long. More pounding resonated through the vehicle.

Who …? Irritated, Corey wiped the frozen steam off the window's interior. Bobbie Be

Good stood outside the car, covered from head to toe in seasonal dress, amounting to a parka with a fuzzy brimmed hood, gloves, sweatpants, and duck boots.

Son of a bitch! Corey had never been so happy to see this woman in the short time he'd known her. He rolled down the window. Steam escaped from the car. He saw the snow was still falling at an alarming rate, but the sun was starting to come up. The black of night had become more of a shade of gray.

"Karaoke Band Man, are you all right?" Bobbie looked genuinely concerned for his safety. "What are you doing in your car? It's dangerous out here!"

"Good morning, nice of you guys to drop by!"

"Nobody is with me," Bobbie turned her head left and right, looking for someone else.

"You've never seen *The Empire Strikes Back*, have you?"

Her facial expression was blank, answering his question.

"Anyway, you are a sight for sore eyes, Bobbie. What are you doing out here?"

"I just got out of work at the gas station. I worked a double; nobody came in to relieve me. So I shut the store down, and I'm going home now. Too tired."

"That's good, I guess."

"Well I saw your car running and figured I'd check on you."

"Aw, so nice of you to do, Bobbie." Corey was watching the snowflakes flutter around Bobbie's head and fall into the car, melting as they hit the heat.

"You're welcome."

"Well, silly question, but did your historian Granny ever teach you about a creature named Neon Harry?"

"Neon Harry? Who is that, someone from your band? Somebody from karaoke?" The puzzled look returned to her face. Corey slowed his speech down and deliberately pronounced the name he heard in his sleep.

"*Neon-Yar-He,* forgive me. My grasp of Onondaga is limited to counties, towns, and street signs."

"Oh! You mean *Ne-On-Yar-He?*" Corey nodded, and she continued. "It's an evil snow serpent. It hunts in deep snow banks, luring men and women with a hypnotizing song. Then it strikes, raping young women so no men will want them, and taking young men as its husbands before it devours them."

"That's fucked up." *Neon Harry the mad flasher, stealing the virtuous, albeit toothless, young ladies and gentlemen of Fenton, New York.* "Well, I think Neon Harry lives down the street from here."

Bobbie started laughing.

"You're crazy, aren't you." It wasn't a question.

"No, but tell me more about this snow demon. The women raping, man eating thingy."

"*Ne-On-Yar-He?*" she squinted as she said the word, as if she'd eaten something foul.

"Yeah, that, Neona Yarry or whatever."

Bobbie's concerned expression turned to one of confusion.

"Have you been breathing exhaust fumes? *Ne-On-Yar-He* isn't real. It's a fairy tale. You really think I believe that mumbo jumbo? Is it because I'm Native American? It's 1993, we don't live in wigwams or teepees and bathe in duck shit."

"I don't fucking know, but I'm here to tell you it's *real*. I'm pretty sure it calls itself Bella."

Bella loves you, Corey.

"What did you say?" He clearly heard the sentence. Bobbie had to have said it. He swore she said it. He watched her lips move, didn't he?

"Nothing, I'm still trying to figure out what drugs you're on." Bobbie's tone changed, again, to one of fear.

"You didn't just say 'Bella loves you, Corey' to me?"

Bella does love you, Corey.

"No," Bobbie replied, stepping back and away from the window, "no I didn't." He heard fear in her voice.

Corey shirked away from her, too.

It's me, Bella, lover.

"Get out of my fucking head, you fucking cunt!" Corey screamed aloud. The outburst was enough for Bobbie Be Good. She turned and ran through the parking lot. "No, not you, Bobbie!" Corey tried to get her to return by apologizing, but Bobbie would have nothing to do with it. She ignored him and quickened her pace.

Snow on the road flew into the air as if a snowblower was working overtime. But there was no snowblower, and no middle-aged man in a flannel lumberjack hat futzing along at a trot, speed pushing the device. In fact, Corey could see nothing except a line of ice and snow dispersing into the air. Whatever was responsible for the event was burrowing through the snow at a great rate of speed.

Hi, baby. Mommy's home!

The snowbank at the intersection erupted. Bobbie Be Good stopped dead in her tracks. She looked back to Corey for a moment, then was jerked away and out of sight by something. If she screamed, Corey didn't hear it. Corey did, however, see the explosion of snow in the parking lot and felt a wave of snow and ice cover his vehicle. He turned on the wiper blades to clear the window.

You shouldn't let stray turtles follow you home, baby.

Snow was many colors: white, most commonly, but often could be gray or even yellow. Red snow, on the other hand, was a rarity. Though it wasn't precisely red, but more pink in hue, with dapples of black mixed in. Because of this, a person may not always register what they are seeing is, indeed, snow.

At first, Corey thought the impact had cleaned his car off. The cherry red finish of his car looked a little off. It took him a moment to realize what it was. Red snow, a hemoglobin byproduct of some person or some*thing*, covered his Cavalier. Corey rolled the window down. A handful of the pink sludge fell into the car.

Ahead in the lot, Corey could make out the shape of Bobbie Be Good sitting, or rather hunched, the fur trimmed parka hood draped over her head. A black pool surrounded her, speckled by the falling snow. She stood up.

How the fuck is she alive? Corey wondered.

Something moved from behind the sitting woman. Corey saw a tendril, lightly glowing with a soft, purple luminescence, dancing around in the air. The falling snow obscured whatever it grew from.

Like a jellyfish tentacle? Corey mused. Recalling his nightmare sent a shiver up his spine. *Is that what Bella really is? A cosmic, space-raping jellyfish-squid thing?*

He watched as a pair of pink, neon arms clawed with wicked looking pincers grew out of the tendril. The appendages hooked onto Bobbie Be Good by the shoulders, jolting her into a vertical stance. Another pair of pseudopod limbs slithered and grabbed Bobbie Be Good's legs by the ankles. The host tendril rose up, and Bobbie Be Good followed, jerked ten feet into the air, spread eagle and arms stretched out. With the window down, Corey could hear her bones snap and crack, echoing through the cold night air.

He wasn't about to sit around and watch this unfold without trying to do something about it. He gunned his car, but the tires couldn't gain traction. The wheels spun, and the car slightly moved. He punched the steering wheel in frustration. The tires slipped in snow and ice, stripping the tread off his tires. He could smell the burning rubber wafting about, mixing with the car exhaust, tickling his nose.

Another tendril, pulsing with red fluorescent streaks, danced around the elevated Bobbie Be Good. She twisted and writhed in the tentacles' clutches as it probed at her.

Corey watched it wrap around the karaoke singer's left thigh. He stared in shock as it tore the fabric of her work slacks away, exposing the woman from the waist down to her boots. He thought of turning his head, but the train wreck unfolding before his eyes was too surreal to twist away from. Corey questioned his own morality as he watched the red tendril drop the ripped pants, then wasted no time in violating Bobbie Be Good. The tip of it struck between her legs, entering her exposed vagina. He saw her mouth open wider than before and her eyes followed suit, appearing as though they might burst from her face. The tendril pulsated and squirmed as it penetrated the helpless woman's groin.

Corey liked it as much as he was repulsed. The singer noted he was getting aroused, again, at no volition of his own. The arousal made him uncomfortable, not from the confined erection, but because of the circumstances.

Who's your Mommy?

Corey's jaw fell in astonishment.

This is what I do to those who try to take what is mine.

Bobbie Be Good screamed.

It wasn't your typical, the *Blob is in the movie theater*, scream, oh, no. Nor was it a baby rabbit screech of distress, so high in pitch it made your skin crawl. This was something different, unlike anything he'd ever heard in his life. It was a low, guttural howl, growing in pitch as if something was forcing all of the air out of her lungs, squeezing them from the bottom. Her jaw vibrated from the pressure, opening and closing her mouth, creating a flagellant sound as her teeth chattered. It ended abruptly with a burping squeak. Bobbie Be Good's farting death throes scream snapped him out of the erotic trance Bella had placed on him.

There was a moment of silence. The woman remained elevated, the penetrating tentacle keeping her aloft. The squeaking wipers of Corey' Cavalier and the blowing fan of the car's heater were the only sound for what seemed an eternity of seconds.

I love you, forever!

A black, tarry liquid projected from Bobbie Be Good's mouth a moment before the red tendril followed out the same exit.

Come to me, lover! Come to Bella! Come sing for me! Bella's voice screamed in Corey's head.

The pseudopod arms holding Bobbie aloft let go, leaving her body to hang on the tendril like a bait fish on a hook. A soft flapping sound floated under the blowing wind as the thing enveloped the woman's body. Silence gripped the air as Bobbie Be Good married whatever had impaled her, and in an instant, she became Bobbie Be Gone. All that remained was an LL Bean duck boot, sitting on the snow-covered ground, listing on its side.

CHAPTER 7

SUNDAY, MARCH 14, 1993 05:36 A.M.
KEY BANK, FENTON, NY
SNOWFALL: 32"

oor Bobbie, Corey thought as his mind still attempted to process what happened to her.

What about Bella? His lover's voice answered, as if she could read his thoughts. No. He *knew* she could. The voice in his head was strong; it was part of him, or he was part of it. Corey wasn't quite sure which it was. Bella, or it, or whatever the thing was, had come after him.

Panic set in. Corey's body shook in fear. He rolled the window up and slid the auto-lock. He turned the key in the ignition. The engine squealed as he tried to start an already running vehicle.

Fuck! He turned on the wipers and defrosters. There was no way in hell he was going back outside to scrape the windows with whatever the fuck that thing was still out there. He tried squirting washer fluid onto the window to help speed the process, but pink ice had clogged the sprayer on his hood. The car windows slowly exposed the outside world through a retreating, crystalline coating. Corey watched as the ice on the windows retreated. *Come on, come on, faster you motherfucker!*

After about ninety seconds, which was far too long for Corey's liking, he was finally able to see out the front window. Without hesitation he gunned the gas. At last, the tires gripped and propelled the car forward, out from the shelter of the drive-thru awning.

Something stood in the snow, blocking his path. He slammed on the brakes, stopping the car. He was afraid it might be Bobbie.

It wasn't Bobbie Be Good, but it was something to be afraid of.

It was nine feet tall, maybe a little more. It was hard to tell when the damn thing shifted and squirmed in the falling snow.

Focusing on it was difficult as a result. It might have been gray, or silver. Again, he wasn't sure. Every now and then it glowed a soft neon pink, blue, or purple. Or red. The snow was making visibility more than difficult, but then again, Corey couldn't trust his eyes. Bella, or *Sbli'rldlnisa-aea*, had gotten into his mind, infecting it with pieces of her(*it?*)self.

Come back, lover. Come home with Bella.

Corey turned the car off. He didn't know why. It seemed to be the right thing to do at the moment.

Lover. Come back to me.

Corey shook his head violently and screamed, "Get out of my head, you bitch!"

Lover. I love you. Sing for me, lover. Sing for me. Sing for the glory of our love. Become part of me. Come to me, lover. Come for me, lover. Your song is for me and for me alone. I've always wanted you, lover. You've always wanted me, lover. You've been promised to me all your life. You are here for me, lover.

Her words sped through his mind, an endless, run on rant on repeat. Corey pounded his head on the steering wheel.

I love you. You and only you are for me. Sing for me, lover. Sing for me. Become part of me. You are part of all of Us. Come to me, lover. Your song is for me and for me alone. You are my love. My only love. I've always wanted you, lover. You've been promised to me all your life. You are here for me, lover.

Corey unlocked the car, disconnected his seatbelt and stepped out into the weather.

She loves me, he thought, *yes, she loves me.* He watched as *Sbli'rldlnisa-aea* unfolded its midsection. A black, viscous liquid resembling squid ink splashed out from the opening folds, staining the snow gray and red. It swirled on the ground before reforming and sliding up on the side of the Bella thing, settling to resemble a bloody splotch.

"... *karaoke* ... *band* ... *man* ..." *Their* voices returned. He now heard Bobbie Be Good's unmistakable off key tone underlying *Them.*

Shit. The voices are literally shit! The revelation reminded him of Bella's toilet and the creeping fucking crud.

Corey's thoughts were ripped back to the present when something lifted him into the air. He saw a tendril extending from *Sbli'rldlnisa-aea*'s body, holding him aloft. Within moments, he was being carried through the storm at incredible speed, ice and snow pellets stinging his exposed flesh.

Then the tendril released him, and Corey fell into a snowbank next to Bella's snow angel, the imprint still visible in the yard at 305 Park Street.

Welcome home, baby, Bella told him inside his head.

Corey fought the urge to move. He wanted to die in the snow from exposure. He dug into the bank to no avail. A tendril plucked him out and dropped him on the porch stoop.

This couldn't be happening.

Corey heard the joyous voices *They* made, heralding his return engagement.

"*... sing ... for ... us ... karaoke ... band ... man ...*"

The front door opened. Corey saw the zombified guitarist and bassist standing in the living room, beckoning him to enter. He stumbled in, falling at the feet of the guitarist. The zombie things smelled of spoiled cabbage and a baby shit smoothie.

"Get up, laddy!" one of the zombies said, a fake Gaelic accent rolling off his purple tongue. The voice, when isolated away from *Them* was more than recognizable to Corey.

"Patrick? Pat Hallenbeck?" He was sure of it; he recognized the fake Irish accent. It belonged to one person, somebody he never thought he'd hear again. Pat Hallenbeck, his high school chum and wannabe stand-up comedian. He was always a better guitar player. Right after high school he'd gone on the road to make it as a stand-up comic, never to be seen or heard from again. It became pretty obvious he hadn't gotten very far on his endeavor, about as far as Fenton, to be precise.

"Aye, lad! Now get in here! It's time for your big break, right Scoop?" the zombie gestured to his undead companion.

"That's right, Pat!" the bassist zombie replied.

Scoop? The old Scene of the Crime guitar player had disappeared years ago on Oneida Lake, about forty miles from Fenton. Famously his body had never been found, but his ice fishing rig and mangled snowmobile had. It was believed an animal had made off with his remains. Corey disproved this theory today. He wondered who in the world they could have on the drums. Keith Moon? Razzle? He twisted his head and saw a familiar face sitting behind the kit. It was Lucas, something forgettable for a surname, a local drummer he knew from open mic nights at various regional bars. The big half-Onondaga, half-Mexican percussionist was a popular fill-in drummer, bouncing from band to band on the scene. When he stopped showing up at shows last year, the rumor was he'd gone to Jamesville Correctional Facility to spend some time thinking about his misdeeds. Corey now knew the rumor was bullshit. He sat there quiet and smiled at Corey, his mouth missing every other tooth.

"Come on, Corey," the thing that used to be Pat said.

"Mr. Karaoke Band Man, hah!" Scoop quipped, Bobbie Be Good's voice resonating under his. Tired of resisting, Corey allowed them to lead him away. The trio made their way through the house to the garage. The singer was surprised to find Bella, returned to her human shape and again wearing an alluring white nightie, sitting on the stage.

You're home now, baby. You don't have to run away anymore.

She was back in his head. He couldn't shake her. The snow had to end sometime. If he could only keep it together until then. But she kept getting into his head. Pat and Scoop may have been too dumb to open the door earlier, but now they had the power hold Corey from running off. They also had the strength to disrobe him and duct tape the singer to a pole in the garage, facing away from the stage.

Corey heard the snare rattle and a single bass drum kick as the percussionist stepped from behind the kit. Even though he hadn't heard it in fifteen years, Corey immediately recognized a voice, and it was not Lucas. It stopped his heart beating for the time it took it to ask a single question.

"How do you add up the number of cows in a field, son?"

Count their tits and divide by four?

"That's right, boy! Count their tits and divide by four!"

Daddy? Corey Collins' mind snapped.

•

SUNDAY, DECEMBER 25, 1978 1:40 A.M. 105 CHURCH ST, APT G, NORTH SYRACUSE, NY. SNOWFALL: 4-1/2"

Lauri Collins and her young son drove through the snow, coming home from midnight mass. The storm started innocent enough with a few floating flakes when they left for church. Her husband, Johnny, had been working late at the bar, unable to make it to the service. She had thought about stopping at the pub on her way there, but Johnny hated when she would show up unannounced. He said it hurt his tips if she came in, so she didn't.

She pulled in the driveway, surprised to see the lights on in their apartment. It was too early for Johnny to be back, or had he shut down early? Lauri didn't think many people would be out at a bar on Christmas Eve in a snowstorm, but she had been wrong before about these things.

Corey Collins watched, both an unwilling witness and participant, as his adult mind saw through the eyes of a nine-year-old boy.

Young Corey tried catching snowflakes on his tongue, dancing about in the snow as he and his mother walked up the drive to their apartment door. Theirs was one of eight apartments built into an old rectory house. A side entrance led to a stairwell and their second floor, two-bedroom flat.

Humid air greeted Corey as his mother opened the door to their apartment. Clothes were scattered about the floor in the living room. Corey recognized his father's work shirt, jeans, and shoes, but the other clothes were new, foreign.

"Johnny? Are you home?" Lauri said, her voice cracking, afraid of what she would find. The dress on the floor was not hers, nor were the shoes. Before she opened the door, she knew she would find her husband being unfaithful to her in the bathroom.

What she didn't expect to find was her husband in their shower, with his head buried between the legs of the other woman.

The first thing to run through Lauri Collins' mind was anger. Not at the act of infidelity, but at the sex itself. Johnny hadn't gone down on her since Corey had been born. She stood in shock and watched as he pleasured the woman. She turned her head and smiled at Lauri.

"*You whore!*" Lauri screamed.

Standing beside his mother, young Corey only saw a woman, her face in the throes of ecstatic pleasure, grinding her pelvis on his father's head. Adult Corey could taste the woman's vagina, feel her soft thighs gripping him. Lauri pulled her son close to her and shielded his eyes. Young Corey didn't understand. Adult Corey, on the other hand, was more than aware of what was happening. He was focused on the woman and, in turn, she was in his mind.

Like Father, like son ...

It was Bella. Bella had taken his father. Of all the stupid things he could have done, Johnny Collins had fallen into the trap of a cosmic succubus.

Corey was no different.

Bella called him, she loved him. She wanted him, needed him, to sing for her. Adult Corey knew she would have him, not then, but *now*.

Will you sing for me?

"I'm leaving, and I'm taking our son with me! Don't be here when I come back tomorrow," Lauri said as she turned, her voice shaking. She took Corey's hand and hastily left the apartment. She buckled her son back into the front seat of the car and drove off. Corey only remembered the snow resembling the hyperspace of *Star Wars*, and the view from the cockpit of the Millennium Falcon, as they drove to his Aunt Betty's house in nearby Bridgeport.

Johnny Collins, on the other hand, didn't know his wife and son had been in the apartment. He never heard her scream; he never saw his son's look of astonishment. How could he? By this point, Bella had already started to consume him, face first. Acidic secretions removed his lips, cheeks and tongue. The gyrating of her pelvis was the only thing forcing Johnny's jaw to open and close. Subsequently, this allowed him to continue to nibble on her clitoris and bring her to squirt more of the acidic ejaculate, melting the flesh off the bone with each orgasm. It didn't matter if Johnny's face had left his skull, he would soon join *Them* and thus be with her forever.

•

SUNDAY, MARCH 14, 1993 06:00 A.M.
KEY BANK, FENTON, NY
SNOWFALL: 33"

"Hello, son. I've been waiting for you. I knew you'd come eventually. Everyone comes for Bella."

Corey watched as Lucas stepped into view, a pair of drumsticks in one hand. *They,* and most importantly the part of *Them* who had been his father, didn't inhabit Johnny Collins' body. His faceless shell had rotted away over a decade before. Instead, Corey heard his father's voice coming from the mouth of Lucas. It was beyond weird.

"You've been misbehaving? Don't make me get a switch, boy." Johnny Collins' voice said as Lucas's lips moved. He brought a giant ham fist up and gently patted Corey on the shoulder. "She only wants you to sing for her. Why can't you get that through your skull, boy?"

"Get out of my fucking head. You're not my father, my father died a long time ago! Fuck off!" Corey spit at the dead thing. The clear phlegm stuck to the undead drummer's pasty face.

Be easy on him.

"Oh, I'll be easy on him, baby. I'll be *real* easy on him." It reached behind Corey with his free hand. Corey felt the drumsticks press against his exposed posterior at first, then his anus as they were thrust between Corey's ass cheeks. The singer's eyes widened in fear.

"We can do this the easy way, or the hard way, son. Bella would prefer the hard way."

The harder the better, lover.

"... *sing ... sing ... sing ... sing ...*" They chanted. Corey saw Pat and Scoop blankly staring forward, their heads bobbing in sync with the cadence.

"Can we get on with this then, son? We've been waiting on you for as long as I've been here. How long's that been? Fifteen fucking years?"

"Yes ..." Corey managed.

"Excellent! Gentlemen, assume your positions!" The drummer pulled his sticks out of Corey's ass and returned to his kit. Corey sighed in relief, but he knew things weren't getting any better.

Pat and Scoop retrieved their instruments, turning them on. There was an electric hum and smell of ozone, then the trio started to play.

It was heavy. Corey could feel the power of the music pulsing behind him. The double bass drums started kicking to start the song, followed by a high hat and snare drive. Scoop's bass thrummed a steady E note in time with the snare. A lead scale erupted from the Marshall stack behind Pat. It wasn't a song he'd heard before, but he knew it well.

It was a song for Bella. A song for his goddess of metal. The music tingled Corey's spine, filling his body with tense energy he needed to release, but couldn't under his restraints. When Bella appeared in front of him, Corey wasn't startled or scared in the slightest. He had been waiting for her. He felt her tear the tape around his groin away, freeing his stiffening cock.

Sing for me now, lover. Sing for me.

Bella engulfed him with her mouth. Swallowing his entire member. Warmth flooded through him and with it came *Her* song.

"*... ah ... ah ... ah ...*" *They* hummed in a chorus. Lights flashed in Corey's eyes, a kaleidoscopic, hypnotizing sequence he knew only he could see. The light wasn't coming from without, but from within himself.

Then the words came to him, if you could call them words. The lyrics were something more, translated into the colors swimming before Corey's mind. At once a ballad of love, and a dirge lamenting what was to come, the song was beautiful. Bella's love was true, but it was also bittersweet. The song of *The First*, sung in his words, had been carried down through the millennia, taught to *Them* by her.

Sbli'rldlnisa-aea, Gudinnen av alle ting,

I damen i himmelen og jorden,

Sbli'rldlnisa-aea For himmelens dronning.

I én som har brakt liv ved loven av kjærlighet,

Du har ført oss harmoni og opprette

Rørobjekter oss ved din hånd.

Corey sang the lyrics, their tongue foreign in his mouth, yet strangely accustomed to them. He *knew* the words. They pulsed with each note, resonating with the colored lights floating in Corey's eyes. He looked down. Through the colored spots he saw Bella's mop of black hair had spread out, covering her back and shoulders, blocking his view of the sex act being performed. All he felt was pleasure and warmth below his waist.

Sbli'rldlnisa-aea, Mor til alle som er.

Vi er dine barn, vi er din ætt.

Sbli'rldlnisa-aea Ta oss til dig.

Forever vi skal synge for dig, vår mor, Sbli'rldlnisa-aea.

Forever vi skal være med dig, gudinne Sbli'rldlnisa-aea.

The words fell off his tongue, entrancing him as they rang out. Corey felt a climax build in his groin and released it, moaning in ecstasy as he did so. Bella rose before him, smacking her lips, a black and purple liquid dripping off them. Corey briefly wondered what it could possibly be, but the scent of her aroused sex distracted him from the thought. She straddled him on the pole, pulled him into her sex. Then she turned her body in an impossible position, turning around on a pivot, wrapping her legs around Corey's head.

Now perpendicular to the floor, she thrust her pelvis into his face. The band played on, laying down a straight forward rhythm he could barely hear through Bella's thighs.

Corey licked and chewed at Bella's cunt. He found her clitoris, a throbbing button sticking through the folds of flesh and sucked on it. Bella held him tighter, bucking on Corey's face. He felt something spraying out of her. Whatever it was squirmed and bit and burrowed its way into his lips and face. He felt the worms tickling his cheeks and lips as they fought their way into him. Agony would have wracked his body, but the euphoria of Bella sitting on his face while she sucked at his groin in a perverse sixty-nine turned the pain into pleasure.

She cried out as she came, a disturbing howl, warbling and shrill. She buckled at the hips and convulsed. Acid sprayed out from her vagina, searing Corey's eyes, face, mouth, throat.

He tried to scream but found he couldn't get the air to do so. He clawed and punched at Bella's back and legs. They held him secure in an iron grip. He thrashed and bucked. A muffled shrill of panic gurgled in Corey's chest, but he was unable to release it.

Lover, don't fight me. I love you. Let me love you.

Corey heard her in his head, and only her. The music was gone now. He felt her legs changing, shifting. The warm skin gave way to something not quite flesh, clammy and moist. He thrashed and punched at whatever it was, his forearms bouncing and harmlessly slapping off it.

Then something dropped down and across his body, engulfing more than his pelvis and groin. Corey found the sensation covered him from neck to toe. It was almost serene. He stopped fighting and let his arms go limp. They quickly found the same bliss the remainder of his body had.

CHAPTER 8

SOMETIME, SOMEPLACE ELSEWHERE...

Corey sat at the bar, a drink in hand. His band was playing over the sound system. He always liked it when he heard Well of Sorrow playing on the jukebox. This time was no different. It was a song off their most recent CD, *What We Lost*, called "Fantasy".

The collection of karaoke characters were all present singing along with the song in a chorus. Frankie conducted them all, waving his hands back and forth like a maestro. Rockin Ron was Kung Fu gripping Sexy Suzie's tits with a reach around, next to Darling Nikki and Doctor Love who shared a mic. Crooked Chuck and his hitchhiking pals harmonized along with the others. Pistol Paull and Big Daddy Vick danced together with choreographed precision, doing their best John Travolta, *Saturday Night Fever* impressions. Bobbie Be Good took center stage, belting out the lead vocals. Corey knew the song well. He wrote it, so he sang along with them.

Hold me, tie me down.

Show me, what you've found.

Super Girl climbs on top of the Man of Steel,

Kryptonite to his Fortress of Solitude.

Lonely, on their own.

The song seemed appropriate. He'd spent the last forty-eight hours banging the woman of his dreams, Bella, a willing participant in a celestial highlight reel of the Kama Sutra.

She's a lovely lady, isn't she son? Corey's dad Johnny slapped his son on the back as he sat next to him at the bar. *We'll have another round of Jamesons down here!* he shouted out.

Aye, aye, aye. It was Pat Stephenson behind the bar, back in his old role, complete with his faux Irish accent. *On the rocks like a pussy or straight up?*

Straight up, right son? Johnny slapped Corey on the back again.

Yeah, Dad. Straight up, Corey replied with enthusiasm. Pat served the drinks, and the father and son downed them. Corey felt the whiskey burn down his throat and throughout his body. Liquor wasn't supposed to have such an effect on you.

Oh man, are you ready for this? It's karaoke time! Scoop announced from the DJ booth. Well of Sorrow and the accompanying karaoke chorus faded away. The familiar riff to Meatloaf's "Paradise by the Dashboard Light" rang out through the bar. Corey found himself on the stage with a microphone in his hand.

He rolled with it when the lyrics came up on the screen. The words came out, pitch perfect. Corey knew this song was a duet. Where was his female accompaniment?

Bella? Will you sing for us?

Bobbie Be Good filled this void, much to Corey's surprise.

Karaoke Band Man! High five!

Aren't you dead? Corey tried to say but found he couldn't. The song carried on for its nearly eight-minute duration.

You know what Hell is, Corey? Johnny Collins shouted out to his son as the song completed. *It's last call, your drink is empty, and some asswaffles are singing this song. Forever.* More bad advice from his deadbeat Dad.

I must be in Hell then ...

Corey was sitting back at the bar. Pat stood before him, polishing a rocks glass with a blood soaked mug rag.

How can this be Hell? Bella is here, with us. Pat motioned to the end of the bar, where she sat, her sultry presence standing out, a living Boris Vallejo painting. Corey saw all her curves and lines, her skin glossy and airbrushed. *We've always been with her, lad—*Bella smiled at him—*and we'll always be. She's the pot o' gold you've always looked for at the other end of the feckin' rainbow.*

A new singer was on stage. Corey saw it was Lucas, singing with his own voice, a familiar song.

Forever vi skal synge for dig, vår mor, Sbli'rldlnisa-aea ...

The bar's patrons, mostly men with a few women interspersed about, sang along.

Forever vi skal være med dig, gudinne Sbli'rldlnisa-aea ...

Forever … Corey repeated in unison.

The bar faded and disappeared from Corey's vision. He felt his body expanding, again.

•

He was back on top of the world, gazing out at the edge of the abyssal nothingness. The lights and colors returned, each a spark of somebody, of someone Bella had loved before him. They swirled and shot past Corey, some stopping and hovering before him before speeding away.

Their voice erupted through Corey's psyche.

"Forever! Forever! Forever!"

Yes, Corey, decided, *it would be forever, after all*, and he lost the desire to do anything but surrender to Bella. There was no use in fighting it any longer. He let himself go to her.

The expanse opened before his eyes, infinite and black but flecks of light racing, streaking to him. The lights came closer to Corey, surrounding him, and she was there, standing before him. Bella, his heavy metal porcelain goddess, naked and shiny.

See me, lover!

The siren allowed the illusion of Bella to fade away. She revealed her true self, *Sbli'rldlnisa-aea,* to Corey. She was glorious to behold, an angel of infinite stars, floating before him. A long, thick, finned tail extended down from the center of the creature, waving to and fro, keeping the chimera afloat. Purple and gray tentacles and tendrils resembling dreadlocks dropped from its translucent umbrella, surrounding the tail. She reached out with her tendril arms, stretching infinitely long, and hugged him. He felt the pressure as Bella held him tight in her arms.

Corey's head lolled to the side and looked down. He saw his mortal form, Bella wrapped around him. Except it wasn't Bella, but her true self, *Sbli'rldlnisa-aea,* embracing his body.

Come to me, my lover …

Forever?

Yes, lover, forever …

Corey dropped to his knees before the creature and fell back into his body. The lights pierced his body and flesh, deconstructing it into nothingness and casting his mind into the abyss. Then he felt the pain, sharp and piercing. Never ending agony inhabiting every bit of his mind, body, and soul.

·

SUNDAY, MARCH 14, 1993 12:00 P.M.
305 PARK ST., FENTON, NY
SNOWFALL: 40"

Sbli'rldlnisa-aea wrapped her tail around Corey Collins' immobilized body, slithering up and around him in a spiral pattern. The scales shredded away any foreign matter on his body. It was time to feed.

She had prepared him for the final consumption earlier as he sang to her. The sperm he released during the oral copulation fertilized her own eggs. *Sbli'rldlnisa-aea*'s gift in return was regurgitated, inseminated larvae. The little worms ate through his flesh, burrowing into the muscle tissue and bones, tenderizing him for her.

The red, glowing tendril, the creature's cervical probe, dropped and sniffed around Corey's body, looking for more sperm to consume. It found Corey's exposed rectum and plunged into it. Corey's head snapped up at attention, his eyes bulging, wide open, his mouth widely agape. He first felt his anus split apart as the tentacle thrust into him, followed by the removal of his prostate and genitals. He felt his testicles and cock suctioned *into* his body and into the suckling, toothless mouth at the tip of *Sbli'rldlnisa-aea's* tendril.

The tendril seized and quivered before ejaculating its contents back into Corey's body. Millions of spindled sperm burrowed into Corey's insides, eating him from the inside as Bella's tail crushed and collapsed his body. Digestive acids secreted from pores along her tail. She constricted together, slapping the stage with her fin. Corey's mind came back to him in the final moments.

That's weird, he thought as he looked down, only seeing Bella's cosmic form coiled about him. A tentacle raised Corey's chin, changing his view. *Sbli'rldlnisa-aea* lowered her domed headpiece in front of Corey's face. He saw Bella's porcelain masked visage reflected in the translucent light. It quickly faded away, transforming into a single eye, a green and yellow orb. The pupil opened wide absorbing the light in the garage, staring at the singer. Corey gazed back, his face aghast. Spiked fangs grew out of the edges of the pupil, creating a gaping, toothed maw.

The optical orifice lunged forward, closing on Corey's head, detaching it from the remains of his body. He didn't notice. What was left of him below the neck had lost feeling long before and was now mostly oozing and dripping through Bella's coils. He found it odd how he still could think as his head tumbled into the creature's digestive fluids and melted.

Satiated, *Sbli'rldlnisa-aea* unfurled from about Corey's body. A black ichor, streaked with red and yellow, fell to the floor of the garage. It bubbled and swirled, gathering all its parts before slinking up *Sbli'rldlnisa-aea's* side.

"… *Sbli'rldlnisa-aea … love unto thee … my goddess … steal … show …*" Corey's voice cried. Her acids had devoured Corey's flesh, bone, and cartilage, but he lived on, immortal and beloved to his Bella as part of *Them.*

"… *Sbli'rldlnisa-aea …*"

•

MONDAY, MARCH 15, 1993 10:00 A.M.
305 PARK ST., FENTON, NY
SNOWFALL: 43"

Sun shone on Fenton, New York and the rest of the eastern United States seaboard. The Storm of the Century had ended. Over three and a half feet of snow had fallen across much of the state, what amounted to about two inches of rain. Diligent DPW crews made short work digging out from the massive storm. Most main roads were clear on Monday morning, though it would be another day before everything returned to normal.

More than a hundred people nationwide had died or gone missing during the storm's tenure. Twenty were from New York, including Roberta "Bobbie Be Good" Webster, who disappeared after leaving work at the Byrne Dairy convenience store and gas station in Fenton sometime on Saturday, March 13, 1993. A boot believed to be worn by her on the night in question was discovered in a snowbank sometime later; however, her body was never found.

When all was done in the world of Man, the former lead singer of the heavy metal band Well of Sorrow would be added to the list of the missing. Corey Collins, not unlike his father, would live on as a Syracuse music scene urban legend, lost before he could reach his prime. As time moved on, his name, too, would find immortality. Not for the music, but for a death, as another statistic of the Storm of the Century.

•

Inside her home, a concerned woman picked up her phone and dialed. Heavy metal music resonates in the background. A tone pulses until a young man's voice answers the call.

"Nine-one-one, what is the nature of your emergency?"

"Yes, this is Sandy Bellavia at Three Hundred Five Park Street in Fenton. My boyfriend went out during the storm Saturday night and hasn't come back. I'm worried to death about him!"

"Calm down, Miss ..."

"Bellavia, Sandy Bellavia. I'm at Three Oh Five Park Street in Fenton."

"Yes, we have that ma'am. Please, calm down. What is his name, and was he dressed for the weather?"

"I'm trying to be calm, I'm sorry. His name is Corey Collins, and no, he wasn't dressed for the weather. He said he was going to the store—it's right down the street from us—for cigarettes and never came back! I'm so scared for him! Somebody help us!" The expression on the woman's face was of a cold wax figure, unmoving and neutral. It did not match the frantic tone in her cries. "For fuck's sake!"

"There's no need to use such language, ma'am," the operator patronized her.

"I'm just off Main Street. It's a gray house." She hung up the phone and turned up the stereo. The opening track of the Well of Sorrow's CD, *Freakshow*, once again assaulted the woofers and tweeters of the speakers. Corey Collins's vocals screaming the song's epic conclusion as the beast reveals itself to the circus attendees.

Big top comes crashing to the ground,

Glad you came to see my show!

My lunar spotlight shining down,

Glad you came to see my show!

Sandy Bellavia, sometimes known as Bella or *Ne-on-Yar-He*, formerly known as

Angraboda, but always known as the Great Old Goddess of Snow and Ice, *Sbli'rldlnisa-aea,* danced. She bent and twisted in place, hands clasped above her head, swaying her hips to the beat of the music. She would wait for the authorities to come and take her statement and then be done with this one.

"... *my love ... love ... me ...*" *They* spoke for what remained of Corey within *Them.*

They were with her, as *They* always were and would be until she was no more. Silent, the oozing mass covered her shape shifted body, mimicking the clothing her prey wore. A new Well of Sorrow patch adorned the jean jacket vest she wore.

Bella's normally emotionless visage expressed pleasure, indescribable joy, at the sound of *Their* voices. Sweetened with the addition of Corey, who would be with her forever as part of *Them,* her skin glowed bright pink and blue. Alternating between the neon colors, in sync with the melody, she danced.

Sing for me.

They did.

...forever...

AFTERWORD:

THE STORMY SETTING OF BELLA'S BOYS

We all remember those moments. Those historic pieces of time wherein you can recite every instance verbatim without embellishing it. Often they're on a worldwide or national level. Events like Pearl Harbor, Kennedy's Assassination, The Moon Landing, the Challenger explosion, the attacks on 9/11. Today, our kids have the pandemic of 2020.

Weather events are often remembered in much the same manner, except they're often filled with added details, warped over time. Countless hurricanes, like Katrina and

Andrew for example. Then there was the Blizzard of 1966, where a hundred and six inches of snow fell on the port city of Oswego, New York.

The weekend of March 12 through the 15th in 1993 stands out as one of the most exciting, thrilling times of my life. The Storm of the Century, as it was touted, came barreling up the Eastern Seaboard of the United States, spreading snow and misery to all. Some of what happened to me this weekend has been transferred to *Bella's Boys'* narrative. Writers often share experiences from their own lives, and cathartic events such as this blizzard, are perfect devices to fictionalize events.

The past few months I had been dating a woman, Kathy, and all was good. I was a young man in my mid-twenties living the dream. I recently moved back to the Syracuse area. I landed a decent job, and I found a room to rent from some dude named Mark on the north side of the city.

The house was a two-story, two-family deal with asbestos shingles painted bright yellow and white trimming about the windows. My roommates were an okay bunch of guys, even if they weren't the brightest bulbs in the bunch. John and Anthony drove school buses, and our other roomie, Mike, only showed his face when he smelled weed or needed to practice throwing darts. So we'd drink beer, throw darts, smoke some grass, and everyone got along. Our girlfriends would come over; we'd make dinners together, maybe rent a Super Nintendo and play some games.

Then the news broke. Less than seventy-two hours in advance. A massive storm, coming up the Eastern Seaboard of the United States, was the real deal. A large snowfall was predicted. The news reports caused widespread panic. The masses swarmed and relieved local grocers of their fresh milk, bread, eggs, and water.

It was essentially a snow hurricane, striking as far inland as Ohio. When it made landfall on the Gulf Coast, the killer storm ravaged Florida and the deep south with tornadoes, high winds, and incredible rainfalls. The snow kept falling throughout the weekend.

By late Saturday morning, unheard of accumulations in a twelve-hour time period had dumped over a foot of it on Central New York, and the storm wasn't ending anytime soon. Blizzard conditions held most of the East Coast under an icy death grip. Thundersnow and lightning could be heard and seen. It was truly remarkable to experience.

In order to completely grasp what a foot of snow is, you must first understand the severity of it. If this had been a rainstorm, flooding would have devastated the coastal areas. The Storm of the Century, the Big One, was aptly named no matter the monicker you bestowed upon it. Essentially a giant tropical depression spewing snow at an alarming rate as it sucked up the warmer waters of the Atlantic and Gulf, it slowly inched north up the Eastern Seaboard before parking over upstate New York and southern New England.

Nor'easter snowpack is typically wet and heavy, saturated with the warm Southern Atlantic water it so eagerly picked up for the ride. Heart Attack Snow, as it was often called, had the propensity of causing overexertion and heart failure in the poor souls stuck shoveling from sidewalks and driveways. Typical snowfalls, from say a Yankee Clipper or even Lake Effect, are often lighter and fluffier. You could blow it off your car in the morning. The general rule of thumb says the colder it is, the less moisture the snow will hold. Twenty inches of cold, dry lake effect snow can be hard-pressed to equal half an inch of rain. A foot of Nor'easter snow can equal as much as an inch or more. Water isn't light when shoveled.

The snow from this was different. The dew point plummeted with the storm the colder it got, sucking the moisture out of it and spreading the wealth, contributing to a longer snowfall as the storm slowly moved. The falling snow became something else. Granular and more crystalline from the cold of the blizzard, it was like sand. It shoveled easy enough, but, much like sand or feed in a silo, it slid and poured everywhere. Soon as a person would move it, more snow would slide into its place. Still, the snow left behind when all was said and done equaled about two feet of rain.

Snowfalls of this magnitude cause quite a few problems, and all of them are, you guessed it, snow related. A square foot of snow weighs about five pounds. Residents living in homes with pitched roofs didn't typically need to worry about rooftop accumulations. The design of their structures dispersed the weight. This wasn't good news for the many house trailers populating the trailer parks scattered throughout the rural and suburban counties could be crushed under the weight.

The roads were another story, and the grainy snow made it worse than it would be from a typical lake effect event. Whiteout conditions transformed them into treacherous death pits. Local DPW teams are usually well suited to handle large snowfalls with their cadres of large dump trucks retrofitted with giant plow blades and rock salt. Plowing through it all and keeping the roads clear is one thing, but it brings up the next problem.

Where do you put the shit? As with any population center, where buildings take up most of your landmass and your storage space, snow storage is severely limited. Mountainous banks from high accumulating snow falls can often become as much of a danger as the storms themselves, obscuring traffic on turns and taking up much needed parking spots.

Central New York was at the epicenter of shit weather central. The I-81 corridor wasn't only an expressway for cars traveling east and west through New York, it was also the carpool lane for storm systems blowing across Lake Ontario. Winds picked up moisture from the warmer lake, and in much the same process as the larger Nor'easter type storms, dump copious amounts of snow on the coastal areas. Syracuse, New York was located in lake snow ground zero, the residents were no stranger to inclement weather.

An inch or less of snow would send most Americans below Pennsylvania into a terrified panic. Large snowfalls didn't stop Central New Yorkers one bit. The Northeastern United States hardened a tough, albeit often cranky from a lack of vitamin D, breed of people. It took a lot to shut the roads down, but this storm did it with gusto. The Nor'easter had only completed the first of three acts in an all-natural production that would continue for at least another twelve hours.

By that time, approximately twenty-seven million tons would fall, nearly thirteen cubic miles of snow, across the east coast.

Now that I've established what we were dealing with, let's get back to me.

I had just started a new job at Bristol Northeast, calling people and setting appointments for a salesman to come out to your house and hock windows and siding. I'd been doing telemarketing since college, and got rather good at it.

My girlfriend worked at the local mall, then called Carousel Center, for the Lechmere chain (think Best Buy, but they also sold clothing). With the advance warning of the storm, I made plans to spend the day at my Aunt Mary's house, which was close to the mall. We figured it would be easy for her to get there in the event of a snow emergency. My aunt loved the idea, helping her manage the snow and humoring my younger cousins, Steve and Maureen. The promise of making snow forts with big Cousin Tommy was the highlight of Steve's week.

It mostly went as planned. Kathy dropped me off at my aunt's that morning and went to work.

The snow started falling in earnest about 9:00 a.m.

By noon the mall closed.

It would take Kathy just over a fucking hour to drive a mile and a half from the mall to my aunt's on Pond Street. The roads were a shitty mess, and Kathy's Chevrolet Cavalier wasn't exactly designed for driving in snow this deep. Oh, and every business in the city closed at the same time as inches fell per hour.

With it being a Saturday, and with the advanced notice of the weather conditions, there weren't as many people on the road. But there was enough to add to the traffic difficulties. Patrons and employees exiting the mall were stuck in a bottleneck for hours. Kathy was lucky, sneaking out before getting caught in the pack, but she still went through hell getting out of there.

Back at my aunt's, I waited for Kathy to arrive. I made the best of it with my cousins. Stephen, Maureen, and I played out back with my aunt's dog Tory, an evil little cocker spaniel. This dog sounded like a chimpanzee on crack whenever you put him in his crate. So getting him outside in the snow was another experience in and of itself. Full of energy, the little bastard didn't care if the snow was deeper than he was tall.

We tossed snowballs; the dog chased snowballs, jumping through the snow. Inside the house, my aunt made cookies. Yes, this was some down home, Norman Rockwell shit. With the added bonus of watching the weather make the immediate world around me miserable.

We downed some hot chocolate chip cookies after shoveling out my aunt's car in case she needed to leave in an emergency and witnessed something remarkable.

Kitty corner to my aunt's house was a neighborhood-sized Wegman's grocery store, nestled at the base of a steep hill. We watched a forty-foot long CENTRO Bus pull a *Little Engine That Could* going up the hill. The bus was about half full of people. It wasn't enough weight for the diesel powered bus to gain traction. The road, even after being on the snow route of the city plows and salt trucks, was a slip and slide of slush. The bus's wheels were still rolling forward as it started losing grip.

"I think I can, I think I can, I think I can!" we chanted until the bus couldn't "I Think I Can" anymore. And slid backwards down this hill.

Through an intersection.

No residences bordered this portion of Pond Street, limiting the number of cars parked on the street side. The driver somehow managed to miss barreling into parked cars or any vehicles approaching the intersection.

Kathy arrived at my aunt's house soon after. She corroborated the road conditions, but ever the adventurer, she decided to chance it. We would drive to my apartment and weather the storm there. We stopped at Wegman's, got beer and food to bring back. There wasn't any milk or bread to be found on any of the shelves.

I lived less than a mile from Aunt Mary's house. It took us an hour to get there from the Wegman's parking lot. The driveway to my house was long and deep, like an alley, with buildings hugging either side. It made snow plowing impossible. There was no way we were going to get into the driveway, let alone get out.

On the way there, we noticed the empty parking lot of the Key Bank on the corner of Park and Butternut Streets.

"Watch this," Kathy said. She drove the Cavalier down the street and pulled it under the covered drive-thru at the bank. We walked half a block up the street to my apartment, dragging our feet through the ever accumulating snow.

Inside the house, the whole crew was there. Anthony, John, even Mike. Anthony had a couple girls over. I've since forgotten their names. The one thing I do remember is that for all of the goddamn preparation we made for this mother of all storms. We got beer; we got bread. We ate frozen French Bread pizzas, and we ate homemade french fries with steak-umm cheese sandwiches. We had all the bases covered, and yet in all this chaos …

Someone forgot the toilet paper.

In fact, there wasn't a roll of paper towels, a package of napkins or a box of tissues to be found. With three women in the house, we ran out sometime around eight o'clock Saturday night. And by this time there wasn't a damn store open. Not that any of us were willing to brave the blizzard conditions and go to any of the bodegas in walking distance.

Nope. Instead, we wiped our asses with towels, like civilized beings, and washed our shit stains off then when we were done.

We were a storm commune. Seven people celebrating inclement weather. The house was alive. Music played, with two TVs on. We didn't care. The Super Nintendo was hooked up to one, and the other just ran the news. Darts were thrown as we played Cricket on a steel tip board in the living room. Others played *Street Fighter II* on one TV, while the other was on Channel 9 and Dave Eichorn.

Dave Eichorn, the legendary weatherman of Central New York, who stayed up through the entire storm to cover it for us. Because fuck it, we all stayed up, too. This was history we were living! Throughout the long winter night, we hung out with an eighth person in the room, Dave, keeping us abreast of dangers at hand. As a result, Dave went on to become a meterologist for NOAH.

Blizzard conditions prevailed. The wind howled, blowing the snow around. Thunder and lightning were heard throughout the night. People were getting around on snowmobiles. By early morning, most of our crew passed out.

But I stayed up. The others came to; the snow still fell, but we were through the worst of it on Saturday night. This doesn't mean the storm was over, by any means. Sunday hit us with lake effect snow.

Central New York lies in a bowl. To the south stand the Catskills and Poconos. The east carries a finger of the Presidential Range into the Berkshires of Massachusetts and the Adirondacks of New York. When wind blows across the Great Lakes, it picks up moisture, and dumps it on the land the wind blows on. Lake effect bands are fingers of snow, little mini-blizzards wherein massive amounts of snow can fall in a short time.

And Sunday was riddled with them. You see, this is the one-two punch effect of winter weather systems in the region of upstate New York. When a Nor'easter blows through, the winds following its path create more snow.

So between lake effect blasts, we shoveled the long and narrow driveway next to our apartment and dug out John's truck and Anthony's Chevette. Well Kathy, John, Mike, and I did. Soon as he could move his car, Anthony took off with his girlfriends on a mission to get toilet paper, he said. They were gone for hours. We made an agreement. Anthony was not allowed to park in the driveway when he returned. He didn't do shit to earn the spot.

During those three hours, we dug out. After making enough room in our small lot for a trio of cars, Kathy and I crossed our fingers her car wasn't towed from the bank. We walked down the street to find the bank lot completely plowed.

And Kathy's red Cavalier still sitting under the drive-thru's cover. Butternut Street, a hospital route, was also plowed. As was Pond Street and their glorious Wegmans.

We pulled in, the bakery was making fresh Italian bread. It was time for Sunday Sauce. We bought a couple loaves of bread, a few pounds of pasta, a bunch of Enrico's pasta sauce, shredded mozzarella and grated parmesan cheeses. We even remembered toilet paper. It was feast time. We loaded up the car with goodies and headed back to the apartment.

And wouldn't you know it ... Anthony parked in the back and took up two spots. There was no room for anyone else. My blood pressure rose, and I promised Kathy if Anthony was drinking, I would slap the fucking beer out of his hand and beat his ass with the can.

Kathy stopped the car midway up the drive. We brought the food in.

Anthony was sitting on the couch, his lady friends sitting on either side of him. He was double-fisting a pair of Keystone Ice beers, smiling and laughing and having a good old time.

I launched across the living room and slapped one beer out of his hand. By some miracle, it landed upright on the floor and didn't spill. The other beer? Oh, I took it out of hand, put him in a headlock and started beating him in the head with the can. Beer splashed out of the half-filled container with each blow. Then he twisted around and somehow got under me. We locked up on the floor, Anthony doing his best to fend me off.

The women and John broke up the fight, pulling me off Anthony. He fell back onto the couch, puzzled as to why I attacked him. He finally went outside and moved his car over so we could all fit off the street.

The Sunday Sauce simmered. Italian spices flavored the air. We ate a hearty dinner and spent another night shooting darts, watching movies, playing video games, and getting otherwise fucked up on adult beverages and weed.

The city was still shut down on Monday. By Tuesday the busses were running regular schedules, and we all went back to work. When all was said and done, twenty million tons of snow fell across the Eastern Atlantic seaboard. In Syracuse, we held the record for the largest accumulations, at forty-three inches in the thirty-six-hour time period. It made a weatherman famous and gave me memories deeper than the snow banks from this storm of the century.

Now, come back with me, if you will, to the time of the Vikings. I wanted explore the fate of the crew responsible for shipping Bella over to Vinland, and their tale follows...

PREY FOR
CHANGE

PREY FOR CHANGE

(Segment from the Lost Vinland Eddas, Varserker (Wolf-Shirt). *Translated from the original Norse prose for the entertainment of modern audiences. Circa 900 A.D.)*

The dragon ship listed to starboard in the still water, unmoving. A white and red sail hung, drooping and useless, from the ship's mast. An arched carving of a dragon neck and head protruded from the bow. The head snarled at an imaginary enemy, somewhere in the mist. A white circle of light hung high in the sky, its warming rays barely piercing the thick, murky fog. With no winds to propel it, and the sea grasses tangling their oars, the longboat was captured. Nearly a fortnight had passed, and now the stink of stagnant salt water permeated everything about the survivors.

Once a flotilla of three boats with nearly a hundred fighting men and women, all that remained was this one long boat and a skeleton crew. Their sister ships and crews were pulled under by the dead things the first night before they learned how to fight them off. Now a dozen men sat on port, hoping to tip the ballast. It only kept the longboat afloat. Two others stood near the stern, hovering about a prone body on a makeshift gurney, covered in blankets.

"She looks like shit, Harold," Garth said, staring at Erica. The girl's face was gaunt, her body riddled with sweat and shivering. "We should end her before she turns. She already smells dead." He wrinkled his nose in disgust.

"We don't know she'll—" The elder of the two men, Harold attempted to speak up in her defense, but Garth bellowed over him in rebuttal.

"Of course she will! They always do. And when they die, they come back and infect us with their venom. Making more," Garth paused, seeking the word most appropriate for circumstances. He spat it out with distaste, as if speaking of them would infect his tongue, "*drowned things.*"

Harold stroked his graying beard. Perhaps Garth was right, no one infected with the venom ever survived. Why would he think she'd be able to beat it? It was a simple truth, her brain would boil, and then she'd die, like the rest of them, but no. She *was* different, and Garth knew it.

"But we don't know how it will affect her. We owe her that much after all she's done for us. Might I remind you, she was bitten defending both of us. She didn't need to do it, she could have let us die."

"That's true, enough, I suppose." Garth snorted, "but what we do know, is the cost she incurs."

"The *Tithe* is more than tradition. It's law. And it's kept us alive thus far."

"If you call this being alive. And how long before none of us are left to pay the tithe?"

"We're not dead, and we're not one of those … things."

"How can you say those words and keep a straight look on your face? Look at her, just fucking look at her. She's burning up with fever; her brain's probably fried from the venom eating her away. Any of the others, we would have killed. You *have*, ended them yourself! But not her. Not your…"

"Not my what, Garth?"

"Ya know the fucked up thing about this? I don't doubt you."

"Then what's your problem?"

"My problem?" Garth paused, carefully choosing his next words, "…it's what scares me the most."

·

Night came, and with it the dead rose from the water to feast on the living. Harold watched as Garth, alongside the others, stood stalwart, weapons drawn and prepared to fight. What choice did they have? The alternative was unspeakable. Anyone bitten by the things joined their numbers.

The oars had been turned around and carved into pointed shafts. Though it wouldn't stop the creatures, it slowed them down and gave the survivors something invaluable: time. When caught on a pike, the things were easy targets for an ax blade. From there it took no more than a single blow to the head to send the things back to the land of the dead. When it's steel versus rotting flesh metal wins, and the rest becomes brain and bone mush.

Torches burned bright about the boat, casting flickering shadows from within the floating fortification. The flames lit up the surrounding area, each a carbon fueled sun making day out of night. The largest fire burned in a copper censer near the stern where Harold remained vigilant at Erica's side, continuing to hope his assumptions were correct.

He prayed, asking his gods for some sign, some assistance. He didn't expect aid. His deities were a fickle lot with little care for the lives of men. If the divine host truly gave a shit about them, he mused, he wouldn't be stranded *gods-know-where,* a thousand miles from home. It was a celestial joke in the form of a shitcake, with a flesh hungry legion from the depths icing the treat.

The stench of rotten, spoiled fish heralded their arrival, fouling the air. The water bubbled and frothed in response, propelling the malodor up from the depths. Harold tasted a gulp of the fetid air and spit out a mouthful of bile onto the deck.

Obscured by the lunar twilight and shadows, there was no telling how many creatures came this time. The size of the rising horde changed nightly. When the survivors heard the wave of the host clawing up the sides of the hull, they could estimate the numbers, based off the dissonance. The creatures themselves were silent, incapable of vocalizing in their decaying state. Their numbers resonated as they moved forward. A wet, slapping sound as flesh struck wood and heralded their arrival. The volume increased as they moved forward, growing louder and louder, building into a deafening crescendo. The survivors readied themselves for the inevitable fight. If the clamor was any indication of what was to come, they would soon be facing a drove like none seen before.

"Shield wall, ready!" Garth screamed as loud as he could. The survivors responded, grunting in acknowledgment, slapping their axes and sword blades on their shields. Metal and wood collided in chorus with a crack like rolling thunder. The Barritus rose in volume to a crashing finale.

Did the gods hear that? Harold hoped in thought and looked to the sky. The soft glow of the moon, hidden behind a bank of clouds, replaced the sun. He turned his gaze down to Erica's prone body. Nothing changed, she remained a helpless invalid, a victim of the poison in her blood.

"There they are! Wait! Wait for them ..." Garth commanded as the horde revealed itself, bit by bit, in the flickering light of the fires. Grotesque, rotting shapes came into sight, lapping at the sea grasses, pulling themselves up on desiccated limbs. Some crawling, some walking on the bodies of others; the things were once men, women, and various animals from land and sea. Deer, bears, seals, and dogs. All part of the rising swarm, all starving for fresh tissue to devour.

Harold noted a seal, dragging its body forward. It ignored the pikes carved from the ship's oars, and along with a dozen other things, impaled themselves as they surged forward. Harold watched Garth and the others swung their axes and swords, crushing the skulls of the creatures, each one popping with an explosion of gray and black muck. As one thing fell, another would replace it. The process was repeated over and over with precision.

"Help! Left flank!" Harold heard Garth cry out.

To the left side, a large white bear gripped a survivor's shield in its maw. It shook in slow motion, with enough strength to disarm the man holding the shield, literally. A funnel of blood poured out of the exposed socket, spraying the survivors and the host in a crimson bath. It drove the things into a feeding frenzy. The man's screams were drowned out by the sound of the feasting. Harold was hesitant to leave Erica's side, but he was needed in the fray. If the defenses fell, protecting Erica wouldn't be necessary. He grabbed his own shield and ax and hurried to join his friends, leaping in, swinging his ax with wild abandon.

Heads exploded. Harold's ax connected with first a deer, then a raccoon. The blows removed the heads from the bodies. They crumpled and sank into the waters alongside the other creatures now re-interned to permanent residences in the land of the dead.

For the first time in over a week, a breeze came up. The clouds above cleared, opening the sky to the majesty of the stars, and moon. Harold saw the throng was spread throughout the surrounding area. He could see what was coming from the water. The other survivors did, as well. The pestilence of fear spread through the line.

It was a kraken, once. Now it was a mass of white tentacles, longer and wider than a boat, with a deflated, flowing body. Wilted pseudopods pulled the thing through and over the masses, covering the host with a white, rippling sheet. Its lifeless eyes were unmoving, but the creature's beak snapped and chattered. Some time ago, something much larger took a bite out of the cephalopod's dorsal fin, causing it to die, Harold surmised. Now it lived again, with a hunger for living flesh.

"So much for Erica!" Garth taunted Harold, "tell me you ended her before coming here? I don't think we need an attack coming from our rear."

"Why would I have?"

"Are you fucking kidding me, Harold? You old fool! Do you know what you've done?" Garth turned and left the line, his ax blade dripping with rotted brain, fish scales, and black ichor.

"Where are you going?" Harold stared in disbelief as Garth walked to the stern and Erica's body.

"To finish what I should have done this morning!" he answered, remaining steadfast in his determination to carry out the execution.

"No, Garth! You can't!" Harold turned to pursue him. Both men stopped in their tracks.

A tall shadow fell upon the survivors, blocking the moon, followed by a deafening howl. Silence gripped the survivors and the ambient squishing sound of the swarm faded. The shadow moved, flying overhead of the survivors, its trajectory arcing into the front of the line. An explosion of wood, water, seaweed, and body parts flew into the air on contact.

"Motherfucker. You better be right, Harold!" Garth cursed. "Retreat to the hearth!" he ordered. The survivors moved back into the boat's center as a cohesive unit. In a few moments they were fireside and re-established their shield wall.

Erica was missing from the cot.

That's my girl! Harold smiled as thoughts of the carnage to come crossed his mind.

•

The dead things squirmed and shambled, collapsing on the ship's bow, enveloping something. Behind them, the husk of the giant squid covered much of the legion as it lurched forward, slow and methodical. A headless body flew through the sky, ejected from the throng. Then another, and another. Soon the sky rained a mixture of body parts. Limbs, torsos, and other bits of gore dropped about the entire length of the ship, landing with a slap on the wood. Pieces of bodies, animal and human, fell and bounced off the surface of the kraken, splashing into the surrounding water.

One of the tentacles reached the crater and dipped into the dead mob. Something first jerked, then pulled on it, dragging the remainder of the kraken forward. The giant cephalopod's hollow body filled with air as a result, returning the creature to its full undersea size. It was massive to behold. The thing's tongue lolled out the side of the snapping beak, which pointed at the boat and what it wanted to eat. More of its tentacles struck into the mob. Each grew taut and stiff, struggling in a tug of war with something.

An evil, baneful howl erupted. The kraken shuddered in place for a moment, then pulled back. One of the tentacles snapped, cracking like a whip. Then another, and another. The air trapped in the squid escaped, deflating the creature. It collapsed in a clump, falling into itself.

A clawed, hair covered hand, still clutching chunks of tentacle shot up through the wall of rotted corpses. A second hand followed, doing the same on the opposite side. A blur of motion followed as something launched forward at the kraken's body. It landed in front of the snapping maw.

The creature was as tall as a man, but not quite a man. Thick, dark fur covered the body from head to toe. The creature's head wasn't quite human, nor was it animal. It was both. The survivors called it the *wolf-shirt.*

Tentacles whipped at it, striking the creature in the back and legs. Twice it fell, but regained its footing, catching a tentacle for balance as it ripped the appendage from the kraken's body.

The *wolf-shirt* grabbed the thing's snapping beak, one side in each hand, restraining it. It twisted, pulling the jaws apart, ripping them out of the squid's body. Black gore spilled out. It tossed one of the beaks aside, then held the other with both in its clawed hands, driving the bone into the squid's face and through the cephalopod's brain. The *wolf-shirt* stopped long enough to howl in triumph; the abominations awaited their return to the land of the dead.

Harold, Garth, and the other survivors watched the carnage unfold from the ship's stern. It was their nightly ritual since becoming trapped in this accursed and haunted place. Once a crew of 30 soldiers and sailors, they now numbered under a dozen, a figure shrinking with each wave. The attrition rate wasn't from casualties. It was a result of their ultimate cost, the *Tithe*.

Harold handed around a small leather pouch, and the survivors drew lots as their battle was fought for them. It was the tradition laid before them by their fathers and the gods before them. If one dies to save the rest, it is a noble sacrifice worthy of a seat in the hall of the slain.

They revealed their stones in unison. Harold saw his was cast with a red dot, the blood stain of those who had sacrificed for the *Tithe* before him. He cut his thumb with his ax blade, and pressed it into the spot, joining his blood with theirs.

"It's decided." he told the others. Garth patted him on the shoulder.

"Ironic, no? You, who defended her from our blades."

"She no longer needs me." Harold replaced the stone in the bag and handed Garth the satchel. He tied it to his belt.

"Yes, she does. Gods bless, as you dine with them this morning, my friend." Garth stepped away from Harold and joined the others.

•

The moon dropped low in the sky. The torches, no longer fed fuel, died and smoldered into embers. Smoke from these rose and melded with the dissipating fog. The sound of the dead had disappeared, replaced by water splashing against the boat's hull and the calls of sea birds. The red light of dawn peaked over the eastern horizon, casting a veil of crimson across the longship. Harold moved to the bow, awaiting his fate. The survivors watched from their place by the stern. A snarling growl silenced the birds. Harold heard footsteps, as the *wolf-shirt* walked down the deck. He stood up to pay his *Tithe* like a true warrior.

The *wolf-shirt* emerged from the fog. Bipedal, it was as tall as Harold, muscular and lean, but covered with a thick pelt of gray fur. It walked on the balls of its feet, and long wicked claws grew from its toes and fingers. The creature's face wasn't quite human, with piercing amber eyes. The creature's maw was filled with long canines and needle tipped incisors. Canid ears pointed out from a mop of strawberry blonde hair on its head.

It sniffed Harold's face.

"Yes, it's me. I come willing." Harold said. "The *Tithe* must be paid."

The creature growled then howled. The cry was a lamenting dirge. A flutter of seagulls broke from a nearby floating corpse in response. Harold dropped to his knees and bent his head back, leaving himself open to the monster's mercy. But it didn't strike. Instead, the creature walked past Harold and continued down the ship.

"Where are you going? I must pay the *Tithe*! What are you doing? I must follow the law! Grandmother! You must follow the law!"

The creature continued to ignore Harold and his pleas, shrugging him off as he tugged at the *wolf-shirt's* fur-covered haunches. It kicked a leg back, striking Harold in the face, knocking him off balance and tumbling to the deck, unconscious.

•

The *wolf-shirt* stopped at the stern and the survivors, standing in front of them, looking at each person. Its amber eyes burned fear into their souls for the eternity of the uncomfortable silence to follow. A collective gasp rose from the survivors when the *wolf-shirt* raised an arm, extended a finger, and pointed at Garth.

"What is this heresy?" Garth asked. "Harold drew the lot, Harold pays the *Tithe!* That's the law." The monster ignored his protests and grabbed Garth's shoulder, pulling him to the deck. It placed a foot on the back of his neck, preventing the man from doing anything other than choke.

"*My law.*" The monster spoke, the words garbled by a mouth full of fangs.

"You're only doing this because he's your family." Garth cried, choking as he fought to remove himself from under the creature's foot.

"*Blood is blood ... Flesh is flesh.*" It paused. "*No?*" It reached down and pulled the satchel of stone lots from Garth's belt and dumped them on the deck. It fished the spotted lot from the pile of stones.

"The gods ... made the laws!" Garth punched and thrashed at the creature. It wouldn't release its hold.

"*Gods?*" The creature snorted, "*They don't care.*" It shot out a hand and grasped Garth's wrist, squeezing it tight. Garth's fist opened up, the creature poked a black, needle pointed claw into the flesh of Garth's palm. He resisted shouting in reflex to the pain. It wasn't the warrior's way. Crying out would surely damn him. It didn't, however, stop

Garth from pissing his pants.

The creature dropped the lottery stone into Garth's palm and closed his fist around it. He flicked his wrist, still in the creature's iron grip, ejecting the stone from his hand. It was a deep red, covered in his fresh blood. The creature picked the stone up, pinched between two of its claws, and inspected it with a piercing gaze from its amber eyes.

"Winner!"

Then it twitched its head, turned it upside down, and looked Garth in the eyes. It exposed all of its teeth with a widening grin. Garth's face turned white with fear. His heart raced, thumping in his chest, sweat poured down his forehead, stinging his eyes. Involuntary tears formed and streamed down his cheeks.

"Are you fucking kidding me?"

"Erica, please!"

"You ... look like shit."

Garth had no time to react, no time to make a vain last attempt at escape, no time to hope for a seat at the table of the slain. The creature stood up, placing all of its weight on Garth's neck, crushing it and popping his head off. Blood jetted out of the stump on his neck, pushing the head forward. It rolled a few feet away, bouncing off a foot of one of the survivors. The creature reached out with a long arm, picked Garth's head up, brought to its mouth and bit into the skull. The pointed teeth ripped through the bone like it was fresh fruit. It chewed on a chunk of bone and brain and swallowed. It took another bite, and another, until Garth's head was devoured in front of the terrified, yet stoic, survivors.

The *wolf-shirt* hoisted Garth's headless corpse into the air, held it high overhead with one arm, and howled. The eerie scream raged and echoed throughout. When it finally subsided, she dropped the dead man's body. Old Harold came to, staggered to his feet and joined the other survivors, not speaking. A long silence followed until the *wolf-shirt* turned her gaze to the others, the lottery satchel in her paw.

"*No ... more.*" And threw the bag far into the sea.

The sail fluttered as the returning winds found themselves captured in the cloth. Erica stood with her back to them, staring at the sky, the breeze cutting through the fur covering her body. It built in strength with each passing moment. She looked at Harold and pointed to the sail, now filling with the wind. This lifted the longboat and corrected the ballast. The boat was finally free.

"*Go home?*" she asked her grandson.

"Yes, Mama. Go home."

ACKNOWLEDGMENTS

They are a son of bitch.

Think outside the box, *They* say. So I did.

Write about what you know, *They* say. So I did.

They had no fucking idea what *They* were getting into.

Born from a joke and then a challenge, the story told was mostly true. Only names and circumstances have been changed, but not to protect the innocent.

I wanted to write a cosmic splatterpunk period piece, placed during the waning days of the extreme, albeit artistic, horror fiction revolution. I wanted it to have a heavy metal beat and I wanted it to be a pop song, all rolled into one. A bridge between the mainstream and the darker extremes of horror. I think I've succeeded with a worthy addition to the genre's annals, but ultimately this is up to the readers to decide.

Thank you, Brian *Fucking* Keene for the challenge. Thank you, Mary SanGiovanni for the meteorological & cosmic inspiration. Thank you, MJ Woods for telling me it needed more … cock. Thank you, Lisa Vasquez for your guidance, Garrett Cook for making it better, and I can't forget Donelle Pardee Whiting's stellar editorial work!

Finally, thank you John Skipp and Craig Spector for writing *The Scream*, a huge influence on the words presented.

This was written to Ghost's library of music, with a focus on *Prequelle*.

Slainte to my beta readers and to my friends appearing in this! As Ozzy would say, "I love you all."

And *They*?

They...

Can fuck off.

ABOUT THE AUTHOR

Thomas R Clark is a musician, writer, and podcast producer & engineer. He is the author of the 2021 Splatterpunk Award Nominated BELLA'S BOYS, GOOD BOY, and THE DEATH LIST—published through Stitched Smile Publications, and THE GOD PROVIDES, from St. Rooster Books. His journalism has appeared in Memento Mori Ink, Rue Morgue, This Is Infamous, and House of Stitched Magazine. Tom lives in Central New York with his wife and their canine companions.